Desperate measures

"Nick, I've got it! For all her liberal views, Lady Brad is a very properly behaved young woman, right?"

"Well, of course she is," Lord Devlin replied impatiently.

"Have you ever kissed her? I mean *really* kissed her?"

Startled, Devlin looked at his friend Ronnie with admiration. "No, I have not. I have been much too well behaved, almost reverent. It's about time a little passion entered our relationship. If she loves me, truly loves me, she won't hold me off." Lord Nick delivered the seducer's standard line with a wicked flash in his eyes. And for the first time in weeks, he saw hope.

DECEPTION
SO AGREEABLE

MARY BUTLER

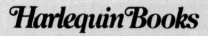

TORONTO • NEW YORK • LONDON
AMSTERDAM • PARIS • SYDNEY • HAMBURG
STOCKHOLM • ATHENS • TOKYO • MILAN

Published April 1986
ISBN 0-373-31009-9

CHAPTER ONE

IN THE RACKETY SET that clustered around Lord Nicholas Devlin, many a young blade had longed for the distinction of being known as the Devil's familiar, but few had gained even the mildest recognition, let alone so significant an honor. Why the friendship of a rake, rogue and fortune hunter should bestow such a cachet is difficult to say. Certainly the glitter of his presence held the same danger as an unsheathed rapier, but that knowledge proved no shield against his undeniable charm. Even the ultrarespectable welcomed him with open arms, most because they genuinely liked him, some because they dared not refuse him.

Sally Jersey like many another lady present at the ball, would have refused him nothing, but she realized she was too old to attract his roving eye and had to be satisfied that he often found her gossip amusing. Oh, well, to be thought amusing by Nick Devlin was no small thing and in the long run far less painful than to be one of his flirts. Familiarity with the rules of amorous diversions—notably their lack of longevity—never seemed to help in his case. In this ballroom alone Sally counted a score of rejected lovers, each with her longing eyes on his splendid figure, offering to return at the slightest encouragement. He was between flirts just now, if it was true that his romance with a certain sultry soprano was now out of tune. After two weeks it most likely was. That half-lidded gaze was probably searching for new prey this very moment.

Sally and the gossips were, for the nonce, very much mistaken. Contrary to his usual habit, Devlin had conferred extraordinary attention, protection and advice upon a young sprig just arrived in town. Although it was popularly supposed that Devlin had no heart, and he himself would furiously have denied its existence, some remnant of sensibility had moved him to sympathy for the plight of the younger son of an elderly, irascible duke, left virtually penniless and alienated from his family.

So now the son of the Duke of Chance gave the son of the Duke of Barrow the benefit of his experience in the beau monde and demimonde. The value of that advice may sometimes have been questionable, but Lord Nick rarely made moral judgments about others. If one had already decided upon seduction, surely it were better to go about the matter with delicacy and discretion. No one could question Devlin's place as England's premier seducer.

"Well, what do you think?" Lord Ronald Graham asked his mentor with a sigh. "Isn't she absolutely beautiful?"

Lord Nick perused a pink-and-white miss gracefully executing the steps of the cotillion. "Yes, beautiful." Neither his expression nor his tone of voice indicated an excess of enthusiasm. Sensing his companion's disappointment, he amended, "Not my type, I confess." No, he liked a little intelligence in his flirts. "But an exquisite face and figure, beyond doubt."

"Yes." Lord Ronald sighed again. "Oh, why is such perfection always unattainable?"

Rarely so amused, Devlin broke into cynical laughter. "Ronnie, you novice, *no* woman is unattainable!"

"She is. Great heavens, Devlin, she's not a Cyprian, or an accomplished intriguer!"

"Women are born accomplished intriguers, and their virtue is nothing but a bartering item in the marriage mart. Once it has succeeded in its purpose—that is, to secure a husband—it is of no further use."

"Well, Miss Ashcroft has not yet secured a husband, and her mama's in no hurry. She means to hold out for the highest bidder."

"Mama, perhaps; but Miss Ashcroft would not be too difficult to divert. By the by, was it marriage you had in mind?"

"No!" Lord Ronnie denied forcefully, laughing. "I ain't that much of a clunch. Not only is her dowry too small for my requirements, so is her brain, I sadly admit. Three months of her would send me to Bedlam!''

"You are too generous. Certainly no more than three weeks,'' his mentor suggested.

"Oh, I am not so easily bored as *you*, Devlin. Nor so fascinating to the ladies, unfortunately.'' He examined Nick for a moment: the strong, handsome features, the virile muscular body, the wicked smile. Mischief had widened the Devil's deep-set black eyes into two polished flints, striking sparks among unwary hearts. Everything about him seemed to glow, from the blue-black sheen of his natural curls to the champagne polish of his boots. In a room full of men dressed in varying degrees of elegance, according to the same strict code, Devlin stood above them all. He was as bright and glorious as a Roman candle—and as dangerous to those who came too close. "You probably could do it,'' he finally admitted, "but don't expect the same success from the rest of us mere mortals.''

"Nonsense, Ronnie! You underestimate your own attractions. All it would take is a little time and patience. And intelligence.''

"You're serious!'' He looked at the famed seducer in disbelief.

"Yes, of course.''

"I didn't think you'd...that is...*have* you seduced young ladies?'' Ronnie was afraid he had gone too far, but Devlin was merely amused again.

"Impertinent boy. No, as a matter of fact. I find unfledged chits unutterably boring. But because I do not want to does not mean I do not know how."

"How, then?" Lord Ronald challenged Devlin.

"You haven't already tried to woo her, have you? That might complicate matters just a trifle."

"I've hardly been able to get near her," the young lord complained feelingly. "A formal introduction, stiffly acknowledged by Mama, and two dances—country dances at that. No more."

"Excellent! Mama has no doubt warned her of your prospects, that is, your lack of them."

"That's good?" Lord Ronald looked dubious.

"Indubitably. You cannot risk her accepting your proposal. But as you cleverly pointed out, Mama is holding out for something better."

"You mean I'm to offer for her? Actually ask for her hand in marriage?" was the outraged reply.

"Immediately."

"But she won't have me."

"Certainly not. But she will come to believe you have honorable intentions. You may even tell her you will not pester her with the offer again. However, after some short absence, you return, pathetically lovelorn, unable to live out of her sight. No woman can resist being the subject of a hopeless passion. It is really only a variation of the old 'promise 'em marriage' routine, but far more effective."

"I don't believe it," said the stunned nobleman.

Lord Nick took the exclamation literally. "My dear boy, I'll *show* you—at least the preliminaries. Even for you, I'll not saddle myself with some Bath miss as a mistress. Now, who shall it be?" His arrogant gaze swept the crowded ballroom. Lady Jersey had gathered together nearly all of fashionable society for him to peruse for his choice. "One must be careful. Never ignore the dangers involved in such a liaison," Devlin warned his astonished pupil. "It is not the beginning of such an affair, but the ending, that may cause problems. With luck, of course, they will realize that silence can only benefit themselves. Fathers—and brothers, too—are far more troublesome than mere husbands. You are fortunate that Miss Ashcroft has no male relatives."

"What if her mother found out and tried to force a wedding?" He did not really intend to seduce Miss Ashcroft, but there was a certain horrible fascination in the scheme.

"Not she! She'd make sure the girl kept quiet, too. I would not put it past her to pay you for your silence as well. No seduction is going to stand in her way to a good marriage."

All this was spoken while Devlin led Lord Ronald in a slow perambulation about the room. Deciding the entire project was a mad joke, Ronnie laughingly entered into the spirit of the game, discussing the qualifications of various maidens. One or two were dismissed as being too desperate—desperate enough to take the rake. Some he knew too well, others not enough.

"Lady Brad!" Devlin finally pronounced.

"Who?" queried his friend.

"Lady Bradamant Mount-Aubin, daughter of the late Earl of Hampton."

Devlin pointed her out to a frankly disappointed Lord Ronnie. Pretty, perhaps, but not in a league with Miss Ashcroft. Oh, she was quite elegantly gowned, to be sure. At twenty-two, Lady Bradamant was free to indulge in the brighter colors denied the debutante just emerged from the schoolroom. The low-cut, high-waisted gown of royal-blue silk showed off gleaming white shoulders and an enticing figure. For the rest, however, Ronnie found her simply average, neither divinely tall nor endearingly petite, neither angelically fair nor sultry and dark.

The more discerning rake, on the other hand, admired the way Lady Brad's smooth brown tresses turned gold in the candlelight and the way her gray eyes reflected her enjoyment. "We were introduced, most unwillingly I might add, by her chaperon a few weeks ago. Her portion is rather small; she needs to make a good match, not an impoverished younger son like myself. Her chances aren't bad, either. Well-born, with a certain panache, Lady Brad has 'taken.' And she knows her own worth too well to accept any man on only the shortest acquaintance."

The orchestra began to tune up for the next dance, the scandalous waltz.

"Perfect. Ronnie, you are about to see a master at work. I suggest that spot by the French windows will give you the best view. We'll be joining you on the terrace momentarily."

It really was a revelation to see how he handled her, the masterful way he cut out the gentleman to whom the waltz had previously been promised. There did not seem to be much conversation during the dance, but Devlin made great use of his special, sensuous look, between half-closed lids, and held the lady just a little closer than convention considered proper. The final strains of the waltz found the couple strategically placed near the French windows, open to provide a little breeze. And as the last note died away, Devlin whisked his partner onto the terrace with the ease and grace of long practice.

Lady Brad was too surprised to protest. This was not the first time something of the kind had been attempted by an adventurous young buck. She had handled them easily, but she never expected to have to handle the notorious Lord Nick. Devlin had said she knew her own worth; Lady Brad also knew that as a flirt she was far below Devlin's standards. What was he up to?

He took possession of her hands but made no advances of a kind that would frighten her unduly. "Don't worry, Lady Brad," he said, to further soothe her sensibilities. "I mean to behave."

These words actually did nothing to assuage the lady's suspicions, rather the reverse. Her expression, however, revealed none of the tumult within. *I really ought to protest,* she thought, but she was too curious to hear what came next.

"There's something I want to say, must say, to you. I've tried to stay away, but it's more than I can bear. Please be patient with me. It's so important that you should believe me. I've never felt like this before. You don't have to say anything yet. Just listen."

Both his auditors attended with growing admiration to Devlin's account of his unexpected possession by a true and noble affection, how he had striven in vain to overcome it, how finally it had overpowered him utterly until he was driven to declare his honorable passion and plead for succor.

If the stars then shone more brightly, the blooms exhaled a sweeter perfume, surely they were conjured to perform by Lord Nick as suitable background for his declaration.

There were no stars in Lady Bradamant's eyes, although when he finally reached the end of his peroration, she wondered if he were not affected by the full moon. Devlin had dropped to his knees, a suitably devout and penitent gesture, as he spoke the magic words: "Lady Bradamant, will you do me the inestimable honor of becoming my wife?" Then he placed a passionate kiss on each of her palms for good measure, an act that helped to wake the lady from her state of amazement, although it could not yet restore her to coherence.

"Oh, please, do get up, Lord Nicholas. I don't know what to say. I mean, this is so sudden. We hardly know each other...." *Dear heavens, I sound like a witless ingenue,* Lady Brad chided herself, pulling her wits together.

Devlin was well satisfied with the effect he had wrought. "Three weeks exactly since we were introduced," he said, as if he had counted the days, "but from the very first, I *knew.* Was I to sit by and let some other fellow, more daring, carry off my heart's desire? Never! I had to speak to you—soon—before too many stories of my past misdeeds should reach your ears and turn you against me. What a muddle! I dare not even woo you in the normal fashion for fear people would begin to talk about you. I want you for my wife; I won't have our relationship sullied by the gossips. Please, darling, won't you say yes? Don't worry about money. We'll manage... somehow."

He gave her another soulful look as he awaited his answer. Lady Brad's look was more calculating. Oh, Lord Nicholas did it beautifully. Really, one could almost believe he had found true love at last—almost. On the whole, Bradamant did not think much of a proposal of marriage that went out of its way to remind her, very subtly, that the man who begged for her hand was an impoverished bounder to whom she had only spoken directly on two other occasions.

Clever. Too clever. He could not really expect her to accept such an offer. No, he could not. So, what then? Damn him! Damn all men!

Looking demure as can be, Lady Brad feigned embarrassment so rich that milord repeated the offer for good measure. Looking up at the French windows, she saw that her chaperon, Lady Bellingham, had come looking for her and had overheard Lord Nick's first and only "honorable" offer. Under the astonished gaze of that lady and Lords Nicholas and Ronald, Lady Bradamant Mount-Aubin gave her sweetest smile and said, "Yes, my Lord, I will be most happy to be your wife."

CHAPTER TWO

LORD NICHOLAS WAS NOT the only one to feel as if he had been caught up in a whirlwind. This sensation was shared by Lady Bellingham, chaperon to the happy betrothed girl. Being much in the confidence of her protégée, she was greatly surprised and shocked by this unlooked-for announcement. It was too positive, and public as well. (Lord Nick agreed heartily.) There was no question of talking it over, giving the offer longer consideration.

A word whispered in Sally Jersey's ear clinched the matter. What went in her ears came out her mouth immediately, a habit that had helped win her the ironic nickname of "Silence." Within minutes, Brad, her hand resting possessively on Lord Nick's arm, was graciously accepting the felicitations of the *haut ton*.

The crowd at Lady Jersey's ball made it impossible to talk privately, but Lady Bellingham certainly meant to have a heart-to-heart talk in the peace and quiet of their home. A gentle, warmhearted widow, Lady Bellingham had originally engaged Lady Bradamant as her companion, but when a timely legacy freed the younger lady of the painful necessity of earning her livelihood, Lady Bellingham had instead offered to chaperon the girl, to whom she had become sincerely attached. Indeed, so close had they become that her sensitive heart was rather hurt at having been denied Brad's confidence previous to the blunt announcement.

She sent away the maid and offered to help Brad out of her gown herself, but that lady was unable to stand still. If Lady Bellingham had not known better, she might have thought her agitation was due to anger rather than joy. She was about to be enlightened.

Lady Bradamant, having finally succeeded in releasing the clasp of her one decent piece of jewelry, a rather fine sapphire pendant, bunched it in her hands and hurled it onto the bed with great force. For anyone still in some doubt as to the emotional basis of her passion, she presently began to qualify further, most vocally. "That bastard! That bloody four-star bastard! Damn him, damn him to the deepest Dantean hell! How dare he!"

By this time Lady Bellingham was thoroughly confused, and, it must be confessed, a little shocked at Brad's mode of expression. As a pair of gold earrings followed the necklace with equal momentum, she managed to interject, if feebly, "I don't understand, dear. Who is the, um, illegitimate person? And what has he dared to do?"

"Devlin, of course," Lady Brad replied, as if it must be obvious to the meanest intelligence. "How

dare he propose to me! Who does he think I am?
Caro Lamb?''

"He couldn't propose to Caro Lamb, dear. She's
married. Even if she sometimes tends to forget it.''

"No, he has another ploy for her sort. But it all
comes down to the same thing—seduction.''

"But, Brad, he has offered you marriage." *And
you accepted,* she added to herself, more bewildered
with every sentence that was uttered.

"Yes, the bounder. Do you want a laugh, Kate?
This should send you into whoops. I really thought
he was better than that. I honestly believed that Lord
Nicholas Devlin, England's most celebrated adven-
turer, womanizer and fortune hunter, had some
standards below which he would not stoop. Well,
how wrong I was! Now, isn't that just hilarious?
Nick Devlin with scruples!''

Instead of laughing, Lady Bellingham was by now
ready to scream, and her cry of "Stop!" was close
enough to an unladylike shout to halt Lady Bradamant momentarily in her tracks.

"Now, will you please sit still and be silent for just
a minute." Brad obeyed. "My dear Brad, you have
now, in your inimitable fashion, left me more befuddled than ever before. I was surprised to hear
Lord Nicholas offer, for once, an honorable proposal, which you, *most* strangely, chose to accept—
after the barest acquaintance! Why you should
choose to do this, something I should never have
expected of you, is mystery enough. But now to rip

the man's character to shreds is really too much! Surely all this is not because he was a trifle... forward?''

"Oh, no, he was remarkably well-behaved, so respectful it was sickening! Don't you see, Kate? You virtually said it yourself; you didn't expect me to accept him.''

"No, of course not. Quite aside from the fact that he is shockingly ineligible—that reputation!—and has almost as little money as you, you hardly know the man.''

"All of which he was quick to admit—too quick! He expected my refusal more than you did, Kate. *Of course* I should have refused, ladylike and demure. 'I am most sensible of the honor, sir, but...' Honor, *ha*!''

"You mean he wanted you to say no? I cannot believe that. Why should he ask, then?''

Lady Brad spared a swift, affectionate hug for her chaperon, her fury momentarily abated. "You sweet, innocent thing! How have you managed to survive so many years in society and remain so naive, so trusting?''

"Thank you for not saying how many years! And how did you become so cynical—I will not say wise—in this, your first, season?''

"You forget, Katy, I spent five years with nothing to do but observe. And since I was to be held responsible for one or two silly fledgling chicks you can be certain I kept my eyes open.''

"That woman! Thoroughly bad ton! I don't know why she's received," Lady Bellingham replied, referring to Brad's former employer with a rare outburst ∩f animosity.

"Probably blackmail, if I know her."

A sudden thought occurred to Lady Bellingham. "Brad, you didn't accept Devlin to get back at Mrs. Bagby?"

"No, to get back at him. Although I don't mind spiting her as an added benefit."

"In words of one syllable, Brad," she begged.

"Very well. Your young rake has a standard bag of tricks he uses in pursuit of his pleasure. Probably first among these is the promise of marriage. You will find recognition of this in Shakespeare, specifically in *All's Well That Ends Well*. It is not new. And it is not always believed. We are not all so gullible as to accept that ploy, especially when the invitation to bed comes first. But if a proposal of marriage, sadly refused, comes first, perhaps some time before any further solicitation . . . ? It works. I've seen it happen."

"Do you mean Lord Nicholas only meant to seduce you?" Lady Bellingham was horrified.

"Oh, you should have seen his eyes when I said yes! You know that look of his, with his lids only half open, like a fire barely under control, as if he wanted to abduct you then and there? Well, this opened his eyes wide! You could not have been more surprised, and horrified, than he. He was so sure nothing could go wrong." Lady Bradamant was getting her second wind. "And I must admit, he's good. I never realized how good. No wonder he's so successful with the ladies. He knows just what to say. Not that it matters much when he looks at you like that, and kisses your hands just so. Perhaps I should be flattered. Most of his flirts have been raving beauties, diamonds of the first water. I'm surprised he even looked at me. Unless . . . I wonder if it was a wager of some kind?"

"Would that make it better or worse?" Lady Bellingham was finally able to get Brad out of her evening gown and into her nightdress. To calm her down further she brushed her silky hair in long, soothing strokes.

"I don't know," Lady Brad offered more quietly, looking pensively into her glass. "Either way, he is going to learn a lesson he will never forget."

Despite the reasonableness of Lady Bradamant's tone, her chaperon and friend was struck with fear. "Bradamant—" she only used her full name when greatly perturbed "—what do you mean to do?"

Lady Brad smiled at the widowed countess in the mirror, the same smile that had struck such terror into the soul of Lord Nicholas Devlin. "Why, Katy, there are only two things I can do now—marry him, or not. Which do you think?"

WHILE LADY BELLINGHAM settled down to a restless sleep and Lady Bradamant to some wicked scheming, Lord Nicholas prepared for some heavy drinking. Unfortunately, he was gifted with a particularly hard head, and getting as outrageously inebriated as he desired would have taken far more concentrated effort than he was capable of in his present state of mental collapse. Unable to bear the comment of his peers (word of his betrothal had already reached the clubs) he sought refuge in his rooms at the Albany. Lord Ronald came along for sympathetic support but was less than helpful.

"I don't believe it," he said for perhaps the hundredth time, then repeated it again for good measure.

"Believe it. I'm engaged! I, Lord Nicholas Devlin, got myself engaged! Dear God, what did I do wrong?"

"It was a beautiful proposal, Devlin," Lord Ronnie conceded admiringly.

"Just the same, no *lady* ought to have accepted it. Why, it's downright indecent!" Like Lady Brad earlier, he, too, paced but refrained, so far, from throwing things.

"How stupid! Her guardian will refuse, of course," his friend offered as comfort.

"Lady Bradamant has no guardian, not even a trustee. She is past twenty-one years of age and has complete control of her own funds. The head of her family, and only male relative, however distant, is the eighth Earl of Hampton, a small-minded and mean soul who refused any responsibility for her when she was orphaned and left penniless at sixteen.''

Lord Ronald downed another brandy and contemplated a gentleman so lost to family feeling as to allow any female relative to marry the infamous Lord Nick. The despondent fiancé also downed another drink, but to little effect.

''Why did she do it?'' he asked himself as well as Lord Ronnie. ''I told you before—she could do much better, meant to do better. Why else would she invest in a season if not to find herself a husband? A respectable, well-to-do husband,'' he clarified.

The brandy was beginning to affect Lord Ronnie's thought processes, and he was finding the conversation a little hard to follow. ''I thought you just said she was orphaned and penniless.''

''Some unexpected legacy came to her when she turned twenty-one. Not much, but enough to finance a season and leave a small dowry.''

Even in his mildly bosky state it seemed to Lord Ronnie that Devlin knew an awful lot about a girl he had met only three times. But then, in their mutual state of financial embarrassment it was wise to be completely au courant with all the ladies' prospects.

''Well, as far as I can see, there's only one thing you can do,'' Lord Ronald ventured.

''Oh, what is that?'' Devlin asked with unrelieved despair and sarcasm.

''Send in a retraction to the newspapers.''

The intent slit-eyed look that Devlin now fixed upon his companion was sufficient to sober the young lord up considerably.

"Jilt her, you mean?"

Why did Ronnie feel so uncomfortable? "Why not? Nobody would be surprised. You don't *want* to marry the girl, do you?"

"No, I don't want to marry her. Tell me, Lord Ronald, if you had landed in this scrape, what would you have done?"

He squirmed in his chair. "Go through with it, I suppose. But—"

"But nobody will expect Lord Nicholas Devlin to do the gentlemanly, the honorable, thing. Am I not right?"

"Well, I suppose..."

"You need not answer. It is all too palpably clear. Perhaps it serves me right. I never cared before what people thought of me, all those meddlesome gossips. And, admittedly, most of it was all too true." He stood by the fireplace, his handsome features as yet unmarked by acknowledged dissipation, his physique impressively fit. His eyes, black and flashing fire, pinned his companion to his chair.

"I have a sad confession to make, Ronnie. Strangely enough, there are some deeds to which I will not stoop. I have scruples." At the sight of his friend's amazed countenance he muttered to himself, rather frightened, "Dear God, have I sunk so low?'' but mentioned aloud in his defense, ''I am still accepted in polite society, you know.''

''Well, of course you are.''

''If I were as low as you seem to think, there would be no 'of course' about it.'' He recited his virtues. ''I am not a murderer. Nor a rapist. Half of my affairs, both those of the sword and those of the heart, were forced on me. I've had more than my share of brawls and duels, but I play by the rules, with those who know the rules. And I pay my debts.'' He laughed without mirth and poured himself another brandy. ''I've even been known to pay my tailor from time to time.''

Lord Ronnie uttered a few unintelligible mumbles that were meant to convey apology. Who would have thought care-for-naught Devlin was sensitive about his reputation? It was true, too. He was no woman's first affair, even second. And among his virtues modesty must surely be included, for he had not even thought to mention his naval experience and heroism under Nelson when he was little more than a boy.

''You mean you'll actually go through with it? Marry the girl?''

''No! Although it would serve her right if she were tied to me for the rest of her life. Damn, I still do not understand why she did it.''

''Well, you know, Devlin, you're quite a fellow with the ladies. Got all of 'em sighing over you. Maybe she's in love with you.''

"Nursing a secret passion from afar? Somehow I just cannot believe that—even considering my overwhelming charm! Funny, just before she said yes there was a certain look in her eyes, as if I were a particularly noxious slug. And when she accepted me, that smile! I felt as if someone were walking over my grave." He shivered at the memory.

"But if you're not going to marry her, and you're not going to jilt her... You aren't going to jilt her?"

"No, Ronnie. Lady Bradamant is going to jilt me."

CHAPTER THREE

DEVLIN NEGLECTED to place the announcement of his promised nuptials in *The Times* in the hope that he might immediately succeed in breaking the engagement. He had considered starting his betrothal with a broken appointment—a good move if this were to be a lengthy campaign. On the other hand, with any luck Lady Bellingham might already have told Lady Brad enough horror stories about him to give her nightmares. A few reminders from him of his wickedness, an obvious reluctance to reform in any way, might finish the task.

Seeing his companion of the previous evening, stretched out on the sofa, still fully dressed and unconscious, gave Devlin the idea of feigning intoxication, but as he had never been seen in such a state before, he doubted his audience would find it credible. He was careful to be annoyingly late, however.

It was a notably unsuccessful ploy. Any other fiancé would have been heartily scolded for such tardiness. Instead, he had to wait for Lady Brad, who was not yet ready. She then took the wind out of his sails by greeting him, as she entered, with an apology. "I'm sorry, dear. I never expected you so early."

There was no sarcasm behind the tone, either—and he two hours overdue!

To his surprise, Devlin found himself responding politely, even gallantly. "You are always worth the wait, Lady Brad. Think nothing of it." Had the circumstances only been different Lord Nicholas would happily have dwelt on the charming picture Lady Brad presented in a carefully ingenuous morning gown of golden-yellow India muslin.

Of the three present, only Lady Bradamant seemed entirely at ease. Lady Bellingham showed the greatest indication of distress, which Devlin took to be a hopeful sign. She was an amiable and most respectable lady whom even Devlin, who held a notoriously low opinion of women, held in some esteem. *She cannot like the match,* he assured himself. If Lady Brad had not been wearing that knowing yet innocent smile again, he might have felt more secure.

The smiling lady held a number of newspapers in her hands. "Oh, Nick, have you seen the announcement? How lovely it looks in print! And see how prominently it is displayed! Nobody could fail to see it," she said delightedly.

Certainly the announcement had been given good coverage. All the journals had it, from *The Gazette* and *The Observer* to some of the lesser rags. Devlin had not bothered to check that morning. Who, he wondered, was the officious busybody who had sent in the notice? Under a half-lidded gaze, he considered his fiancée for a moment, but then declared her innocent. Lady Brad seemed to assume he had done it, and there did not seem to be any point in accusing anyone else.

Lady Bellingham had been surprised as well to see the notice appear so quickly, but she had not observed Brad taking the time to send off the messages directly from Lady Jersey's ball during a supposed trip to the ladies' retiring room. Not that it mattered. Even without the formal announcement, the gossip had undoubtedly reached every household in the *haut ton*. Silence Jersey could account for more than three-quarters of the beau monde herself.

Lady Brad's innocent pleasure in society's attention gave Devlin hope and a hint of the first direction to try. After all, the earl's daughter had spent five years rejected by the ton, forced to earn her living in the humiliating role of lady's companion. Having finally reached a position of some prominence, especially now that she had the prestige of having attached him, surely she could not throw it all away by keeping him?

Devlin smiled, looking up from the notice. "I hope you mean to give us a bang-up party to send us off, Lady Bellingham."

The countess looked a little perplexed. This did not sound like a man seeking escape. She cast a frightened glance toward Bradamant for guidance, but the young lady merely beamed with wicked glee.

"An engagement party?" Lady Bellingham dithered. "Well, of course, I could never let such a big moment in my dear Brad's life pass without celebration."

Devlin, noting her confusion, misread it as a sign of her disapproval—rather than her doubt as to whether, in fact, they were engaged—and took heart.

"Since it will be the last party for Brad for some time, I'd like her to have something really lovely to remember." He smiled genially, waiting for the storm to break.

Lady Bellingham responded on cue "Last party? I don't understand."

He turned, waiting for Lady Brad to add a more peremptory request for further elaboration. He was doomed to disappointment.

"Nick and I will be living very modestly, Kate," Lady Brad explained gently.

She was taking this far too well for Devlin's peace of mind. Perhaps she did not quite understand. "*Very* modestly," he emphasized. "In fact, I doubt we'll be able to come up to town for some time."

"I'd forgotten you had that place in the country." Lady Bellingham tried to remember. "Now, where was it?"

"In Yorkshire," he informed her with malicious delight. "*North* Yorkshire."

"Oh." She tried quickly to cover her dismay. "Well, I believe they have quite a respectable society in York. And some very elegant assemblies."

"We are not at all near the city."

"I expect that when it snows we won't even be able to get to the village." Brad laughed with unimpaired goodwill. The prospect did not seem to worry her unduly.

Devlin's heart grew cold with fear. He shifted his tactics to mere delay. "Of course, I do not know in what condition the place may be. I suspect it needs a great deal of work to make it ready for my bride." He wished he had phrased that differently. Calling Lady Brad "my bride" seemed so terribly final, as if it were all true, and not just a nightmare.

"Make it ready for me? And spoil my fun? Never," she teased, striking further terror into his heart. "It's not many women who get to build their homes from scratch. I shall have a marvelous time. And by freeing you from domestic details, I will enable you to devote all your energies to the really important work of putting the land into better shape."

Must she be so damnably cheerful—and reasonable? He gritted his teeth and managed a fairly carefree laugh. "Far be it for me to deprive you of any pleasure, my dear. But I do think we'd best make sure first that we will, in fact, have a roof over our heads when we get there. As soon as the season ends I will—"

"The vicar" was Lady Bellingham's unexpected interruption.

While Lord Nick looked confused (he had little contact with the clergy), Lady Brad caught her drift immediately.

"Of course—the one person who can give a true picture of the situation. Nick, you must write the local vicar to find out how things stand. He will be so delighted you are finally taking an interest in the area he will go out of his way to be helpful."

"That's a wonderful idea. Only, how do I find out who he is?"

Both the ladies laughed. "Since the living is undoubtedly in your gift, I expect your London man of affairs could tell you. You use Kellogg, don't you?"

"Yes."

"Good, so do we. I'm sure that will make the marriage settlements so much easier." Before Devlin could control an instinctive shiver, Lady Brad continued breezily, "But we don't want to talk about anything so crass as money."

Poor Lord Nick. That instinctive shudder had not gone unnoticed—by either lady. While Brad was glad to see him squirm, Lady Bellingham was horrified. Was it possible that Brad was right? That far from being an eager bridegroom Devlin was a wicked seducer trying to wriggle out of the connection? Kate's gentle heart was stirred to unaccustomed anger. He deserved to squirm.

"No, we have much more important things still to settle. Brad, my social calendar is right there on the desk.... Oh, thank you, Nicholas." Lady Bellingham smiled sweetly at the victim and perused the volume carefully. "There." She pointed to a date three months hence, at the end of the season. "That will give us just enough time to prepare a truly lovely wedding—a day to remember all your lives—without keeping impatient lovers apart longer than necessary."

"Perfect," Brad said with joy, realizing she had acquired an ally. "And we can have our party just the week before."

Nick obviously had nothing to say—indeed, he could not even think of anything. His mind had gone blank, except for the whisper of hope that said he still had three months to think of something.

"My poor dear," Brad sympathized to a surprised Devlin as she escorted him to the door. *Good heavens,* he thought, *pull yourself together! She does not know.* "You must not worry, Nick." He regarded her warily. "I know all the preparations sound positively frightening, but I won't let them come between us." She squeezed his arm encouragingly.

"I never realized there was so much...fuss...to getting married," he choked out.

"I know. Isn't it dreadful? But Kate and I will try to spare you as much as we can. And I promise I will keep Katy under control. After all, the wedding is not as important as being married."

"You are a very wise woman, Brad. I do not know what I did to deserve you."

"Don't you? I am punishment for all your past sins. And you'll have to pay for the rest of your life."

She said it as a joke, but to Lord Nicholas it sounded ominously like a threat.

DEVLIN FELT like a leashed animal as he left the Bellingham town house. He was free for that evening, but he was beginning to feel the pull on his collar. Both ladies had taken his escort for the remainder of the season's social events quite for granted. His presence was commanded the next day to choose a ring and to see the date reserved and banns called at St. George's in Hanover Square.

Churches always made Lord Nick extremely nervous.

At his chambers he found a note from a hung-over Lord Ronald saying he would meet him later that evening at White's. Devlin would have much preferred to postpone facing the world until he felt himself to have some control over the situation, but as such embarrassing attentions were inevitable, he might as well get it over as soon as possible. The ton must never know that he had fallen into his own trap. They, too, as well as Lady Brad, must firmly believe in his desire to wed.

So he accepted all the congratulations and gibes with a merry smile and a gentle quip and with fierce determination in his heart. Alvanley teased him for being caught at last, and he agreed with seeming delight.

"Well and truly caught. There has never been a more willing prisoner," he lied.

He ordered champagne for everyone. "You shall toast my good fortune. I'll hear no snide remarks. All negative comment shall be recognized for what it truly is—sheer, unadulterated jealousy."

Every member of the club had something to say to him, and even more to say among themselves. That the Devil should marry at all was a shock to the system; that he should ally himself with a well-bred, strong-minded girl of merely passable good looks and small fortune was positively shattering. Half of them, in spite of the announcement in the society journals, had thought it all a mistake until he confessed so cheerfully. They gaped openly and stared surreptitiously, and discussed in great detail what he could possibly see in the girl. Some who were more sensible, of course, pondered instead what an intelligent, virtuous girl could see in so notable a rake. Would he reform? Was is a ruse, a protection against some more clever, scheming female, to be called off when necessary? The possibilities for gossip, and wagers, were endless. Already recorded in the betting book was one wager on whether the wedding would ever take place, and it was soon joined by another on how soon it would be called off, and by whom.

Devlin restrained Lord Ronald from expressing astonishment at the Devil's handling of his predicament. There was little chance for them to speak at all, in any case, with the crowds of well-wishers and jokesters. His cheerful insouciance was suddenly tried by the sound of a snide, insinuating tenor voice emanating from a presence by his left ear.

"Well, Cousin, so you're getting leg-shackled at last! I never thought to see you caught in parson's mousetrap—certainly not by any chit worth less than twenty thousand pounds per annum."

Lord Nick's heavy-lidded eyes narrowed with caution and distaste. Considering his own checkered past, Devlin rarely passed judgment on others, but his cousin, Sir Lucien Rendall, baronet, he freely and openly characterized as the lowest sort of toad. Although the relationship was distant, some traces of the Devlin charm might be seen in the tall figure of the older man, but malice had hardened the even features into disagreeable lines and a permanent sneer.

"It would be useless to explain to you, I know, that there is more to any person than his title and bank balance. I had thought, however, that you might have learned to keep your conclusions to yourself." He referred to Rendall's indiscretion in once openly disdaining Beau Brummell early in his career as *arbiter elegantiarum*. As a result of that encounter, Sir Lucien preferred to spend his time as a leader of county society rather than to be a very minor cog in London's *haut ton*.

"Why have you graced the metropolis with your presence?" Lord Nick wondered aloud. "I thought you were kept too busy playing errand boy for my illustrious parent, though why you bother I cannot guess. Not that I doubt in the least that his grace will leave every possible unentailed acre and penny away from his disappointing offspring, but, you see, there is sadly very little that is unentailed."

The smiles they exchanged were more like wolves baring their fangs.

"I'm hurt, Cousin, that you should so misunderstand my deep affection for your noble sire. After all, your family are all the relatives I have. Just because you are lacking in family feeling—"

"Just because I am not willing to be a human doormat?"

"How I hate to see these family rifts and misunderstandings! In fact, it is on a mission of peace and paternal concern that you find me."

Devlin's brows tilted wickedly. "My father wishes to be conciliating and sends *you* to intercede with me?" His tone was skeptical.

"Alas, my lord, not to you. Although I'm sure he would if he felt my chance of success to be at all feasible," he assured the uninterested peer. "No, I'm off to India on his behalf."

Only the slightest tension of Lord Nick's spine indicated his now complete attention. "I doubt you will have better luck with Charlie. You thought him a slow-top, but he was always swift enough to see through you."

"But I go only to assist Lord Welting in accomplishing his own desires," Rendall protested. "He has long discussed sending his eldest children back to England for some town bronze now that they are old enough."

"Discussed with whom? To my certain knowledge he and the duke have not corresponded for...oh, it must be close to twenty years now. And yet you think he would trust his children to your tender care and that of the duke's? I had not thought his grace to be so foolish, but perhaps he has grown desperate."

"The duke is no fool. He would not send me on a useless voyage, I assure you."

"His grace has always tended to underestimate his sons; however, I am sure you will have a fascinating trip nonetheless."

"My only regret is that I fear I will miss your nuptials. I hear the date is already set?"

"Three months hence. I will remember that it will not be necessary to send you an invitation."

"Such a pity your brother will miss it as well! May I carry any messages to him for you?"

"Give them all my love and good wishes." Nick would not give Rendall a chance to read his private correspondence. He would send the explanation of his present predicament by more trusted hands.

"Of course. And my best wishes to you and Lady Bradamant."

Tension finally eased upon the baronet's departure. More members entered the club room to offer their felicitations and ribald advice until Devlin could take no more. The surprise of his upcoming wedding was easier discussed behind his back anyway, so he left to enjoy some fresh air, accompanied by Lord Ronald.

THEY WERE SILENT for some time, Lord Nicholas needing to walk off his ill humor and Lord Ronnie wishing to be tactful without knowing what comfort to offer. Finally he said, diffidently, "So you set a date?"

"I set a date! *I* did absolutely nothing. I sat there mum as an oyster while two gentle ladies rearranged my future. Dear God! Never in my life have I felt so...so helpless. They just went on and on. And I could not think of a damn thing to stop them!"

"I thought Lady Bellingham would be on your side. I mean, against the marriage."

"So did I. In fact, at the beginning she looked as uncomfortable as I felt. Then suddenly she seemed to change her mind—after I had done my best to depict a desolate life of dire poverty and social isolation, too!"

"Lady Brad wasn't taken aback?"

"Taken aback? My dear boy, she is all ready to repair the Devlin family fortunes. What's worse, I believe she could do it—single-handedly! The man doesn't exist who can hold his own against her! I may take her to Yorkshire, if I hear that the property is in a sufficiently depressing state, but I am not at all sure that even an utterly derelict manor will daunt her.''

Lord Ronald shook his head despairingly. ''She must be in love with you, Nick. A woman would have to be absolutely dotty to want that sort of life—either dotty or desperate.''

Devlin seemed to expand before Lord Ronnie's eyes, adding at least a foot to his already impressive height. The young nobleman had never seen this menacing aspect of his friend before. This was a man who well deserved the appellation Devil.

Deadly still, Lord Nick emphasized, ''Lady Bradamant Mount-Aubin is a lady of recognized merit and virtue, admired by Brumell for her panache, by Mrs. Drummond-Burrell for her spotless reputation and genteel behavior. While her dowry is small, she is far from destitute, and she is more than capable of seeing to her future herself. In no way could she be considered desperate for a husband.''

''No, Nick, I didn't mean that,'' Lord Ronald apologized, horrified at the thought that he might have accidentally impugned the lady's honor. ''I was thinking of... of the conditions of a will, something like that. You know, she could only inherit some fortune if she was married by a certain date or... or something.''

Devlin came off his high ropes just slightly. ''Don't I keep telling you she is hardly desperate? In the club *two* fellows—Wibberly and Jack Ransom—confessed they'd offered and been refused! Both of them eminently respectable and quite well-to-do.''

"Now, Nick, a girl would have to be desperate to take old Wibberly. Most boring man in the city of London, I assure you!"

"And Ransom? For all I know there may have been more."

They remained silent, pondering the strange insanity of an intelligent woman wishing to ally herself with Nick Devlin, until they were once more comfortably settled in Devlin's chambers, brandy in hand.

"What are you going to do?"

"I'm not sure." Devlin sounded tired. "I still can hardly take it in. It simply makes no sense. For five years, before an unexpected legacy saved her, Lady Brad was penniless, forced to work for people like that toad-eating social climber Drusilla Bagby just to stay alive. You would think she'd do almost anything to avoid facing that kind of penny-pinching existence again."

Lord Ronald considered the matter, more carefully and intelligently than before. "Well, you know, Nick, maybe it doesn't really look so bad to her. You have the land. Maybe it is in bad shape now, but that doesn't mean things will always be bad. Now, what if you could show her that you were such a spend-thrift, a gambler, that you were likely to lose it all . . . ?"

"Not bad, not bad. The only problem is how much can I afford to lose?"

"Lose to me. I'll give it back," he offered generously.

"Ronald, no one in his right mind could possibly believe that I might lose to you in any sporting proposition. No offense. And I dare not take anyone else into my confidence."

"I see. You couldn't lose at cards at all, anyway. It would have to be roulette."

"Which I have always despised."

"Or wagers."

"A possibility," Nick conceded. "But I cannot let it appear that I have lost all judgment."

"You can go on a buying spree, too—new togs for the wedding, gifts for the bride and so on."

"Yes, but again, how much do I have to lose or spend to frighten her enough to call the engagement off? It will do me little good to find myself free of Lady Bradamant but held in debtors' prison."

"You might make it appear worse than it really is. Try to borrow some money from her," he cried, inspired.

"That is also a possibility—as long as no one can prove it false."

"You need really only show how truly you deserve your reputation."

"Yes," Nick agreed hesitantly. "Not immediately, however. I'm madly, honorably in love, remember? The very fact that I have proposed marriage at all proves it. Some things I can continue, but that which Lady Brad would undoubtedly think the worst and unforgivable—other women—would not look right, would not make sense, yet.''

"What about that opera singer you had in keeping?''

"Unfortunately, Sirène, being far more concerned with financial matters than my lady, decided to bestow her favors on a vulger, but oh, so wealthy cit. As it happens, we went our separate ways shortly after I first met Lady Brad.''

"What an awful coincidence.''

"Isn't it? Oh, well, I suppose I can still appear a hopeless flirt, in a more general and less purposeful way. But for all you say she must love me, Lady Brad hardly seems the jealous, overly possessive sort. You know,'' he realized all at once, "she has never said that she cares for me at all.''

"Women are strange,'' Lord Ronald commented wisely. "Have you ever been in love, Nick?'' he dared to ask, emboldened by brandy.

"Me? Heavens, no! But I have seen it happen,'' he admitted. "The real thing. And you are absolutely right, it does make people behave very oddly.''

They both considered the strange phenomenon of a woman in love, passing the brandy bottle around once more. Alcohol had the effect of sharpening Lord Nick's wit.

"Danvers! He was jilted, only days before the wedding, too. Why?''

"That's right, you'd not have heard in town. His father paid pretty heavily to keep it quiet. I only found out because one of our footmen was related to the girl. The bride discovered her maid was increasing . . . by guess who?"

"Careless of him, I must say. And rather extreme for me, I think."

"Rather," his friend agreed. "Who else do we know that's been given the boot? Tregarth, Kenniston, Lord Cherville."

"All right, what quality did they possess that so enraged, saddened or disgusted their betrotheds that they were returned their rings and shown the door?"

"Well, Tregarth's obvious. He returned home from the peninsula minus an arm and the silly miss couldn't bear to look at him."

"Or be seen with him. Socially embarrassing, what? Not very helpful. I doubt Lady Brad would believe any tale of illness in the first place, and certainly would not turn aside if she did. She would never desert a man when he most needed her."

"Heredity!" cried Lord Ronald, inspired again. "Madness in the family!"

"Now, there you may have something. She cannot have considered, cannot have realized that by marrying me she becomes part of a family that contains a worm like Sir Lucien Rendall. And, of course, there is my illustrious sire, his grace the Duke of Chance." He considered his parent in grim silence. "Really, Ronnie, don't you think, as a dutiful son, I ought to present Lady Brad to the duke?'' His mood lifted suddenly and he laughed. ''By God, I would love to see it. Once, just once, I'd like to see him meet his match. And if anyone can stand up to the duke, that person is Lady Bradamant Mount-Aubin! Yes, I will take her to Chance! The very air there seems to breed quarrels. What else?''

''Kenniston was told by his lady that she had concluded they 'would not suit' after all.''

'' 'Would not suit'? What the devil does that mean?''

''I don't know.'' He shrugged. ''They didn't agree, I suppose.''

''That's another meaningless phrase, 'didn't agree.' Or no, perhaps it is not. If Lady Brad and I were to quarrel over a matter of basic principle . . . ?''

''Like the Whig reforms!''

Devlin removed the brandy bottle from his friend's reach. ''I hardly think one need be reduced to politics. Religion, perhaps.''

''How to raise children.''

''How many we have.''

''Free love.''

''How I expect my lady wife to behave. Reformed rakes often make the strictest husbands.''

Feeling much more cheerful, the young men chatted, with some further recourse to the decanter, until Lord Ronald was snoring on the sofa as he had done the previous evening. Thus undisturbed, Devlin scratched the following private list in his memorandum tablet: "Bad habits—women/gambling/overspending/evil haunts and companions. In-laws/Chance/successful rival/difference of opinion."

Lord Nicholas had never before failed to get what he wanted from a woman. He saw no reason why he should not still succeed and gain his freedom from Lady Bradamant.

CHAPTER FOUR

THE NEXT DAY found Lord Nicholas in the uncomfortable situation of having to confer with the clergy, making arrangements for a wedding he devoutly prayed would never take place. The interview had, for him, a terrible nightmare quality. Lady Bradamant clung to his arm and smiled into his eyes in a sweetly affectionate manner that he could not quite believe in. But while the pastor reserved the date and hour for the wedding, and discussed music with Lady Bradamant, Devlin finally realized that unless he worked like a slavey there was a strong possibility that three months would find him once again at St. George's, Hanover Square, swearing away his future and his freedom.

From there Lord Nicholas went with his betrothed—he was not at all sure who took whom—to Rundell and Bridges to choose a betrothal ring. Devlin, as a notorious womanizer, was hardly unfamiliar with that august establishment. Trinkets he had purchased there had pleased countless amorous ladies and courtesans. But trinkets they were, no more. Such were the attractions of Lord Nicholas that his lovers were often far more concerned with trying to hold his wandering attention than with trying to prize costly gifts from his purse. Now Mr. Rundell presented a tray for their inspection, one that surely must contain his most costly wares. It was all very well for Lord Ronald to say he must seem to be utterly spendthrift, but it was perilously close to quarter day, and until that day arrived he had precious little to be spendthrift with. Not that he would have very much more after that. He used to be able to count on winning enough at the tables to carry him over, but since he almost always won he could rarely find anyone to take him on now for more than petty sums.

"Will it be diamonds, milord?" Mr. Rundell asked. "Or perhaps a ruby or emerald? This particular stone is very fine." He held up an emerald of great size and beauty and slipped it on the slim ring finger of Lady Bradamant's elegant hand.

"Yes, it is a good stone," Devlin agreed, "but just a little too large, don't you think? Lady Bradamant has such lovely, delicate hands. We don't want anything too overpowering, do we, dear?" he asked, half afraid she might disagree strenuously. "Perhaps your birthstone, darling?" he suggested hopefully, knowing it to be a paltry peridot.

"What a lovely thought, Nick, dear. But, peridot or emerald, green does not really suit me. I thought we might like a sapphire."

So the sapphires were brought forward. Lady Bradamant proved to have a wonderful eye for quality, much admired by the jeweler. At first Devlin was relieved to see his fiancée reach for a ring reasonable in size, but that relief was soon dissipated by the shop owner's comments.

"Ah, you are a knowing one, if I may say so, Lady Bradamant. I fancy you'll not find a better stone in all London for color, cut and brilliance. Too many fools look at size alone." He slipped the ring on her finger, by chance a perfect fit.

She held up her hand to the light, admiring the way the ring sparkled and glittered on her finger. If Devlin could have thought of a disparaging remark he would certainly have made it, but unfortunately for his pocketbook, there was nothing he could honestly, or reasonably, say. It was a beautiful ring and well suited to his betrothed. It was also likely to leave Lord Nicholas near bankrupt. He could afford it— just—but how many more expenses was this engagement likely to cost him? Oh, well, he thought as he wrote the draft on his bank, Lady Bradamant was not the kind to retain the ring after she ended the alliance, as he hoped would happen.

After this important purchase was made it was, of course, necessary that the happy couple join the fashionable promenade in Hyde Park so that Lady Brad could flaunt her acquisition. Devlin, who rather felt as though he were being flaunted in much the same manner as the ring, was at least most happy to remove his fiancée from the vicinity of the shops, for fear she should start hinting for a gift of some sort.

Since they were, for the time being, on foot, the affianced couple had no protection from the hordes of well-wishers. With a mind to the list reposing in his breast pocket, Lord Nicholas freely allowed his sensual gaze to rest on any and all of the parading beauties, and even indulged in a deliberately indiscreet nod to Little Harry in her opulent blue silk-lined carriage. He could hear the laughing advice to Lady Brad to keep him on a short leash, to lock him in at night, never to trust him out of her sight.

"He is incorrigible," Lady Brad cheerfully agreed, "but even Nick will find it difficult to find much amusement of that kind in the wilds of Yorkshire."

Devlin had to disabuse her of that idea at once. "My dear Bradamant, I do not find amusement, I create it. It simply exists wherever I am."

Still, she laughed. "Well, no one can say I haven't been warned in advance! But I am not worried, dear." She turned her limpid gaze on Devlin and fixed her eyes on his in a most disconcerting fashion. "Because, you see, I believe that you are capable of anything, absolutely anything...even honesty and fidelity."

Devlin had noted before this upsetting ability of Lady Brad's to remind him, most uncomfortably, of his remaining scruples. Facing her clear, unblinking gaze, he wondered if she truly believed in him. Of all the deep and varying emotions the rakish Devil had inspired in members of either sex, faith and trust were new to him. In all his life only his brother, and in a lesser degree his sister-in-law, had ever believed in him as a person. Surprised into sincerity, he reminisced, ''Charlie always said I'd end up an admiral if I stayed in the navy.''

''Well, thank heaven you did not. I would not like a husband away at sea for most of the year, even if it did mean you were far from temptation as well. But I suppose you could conjure up sirens and mermaids at will?''

''Certainly.'' He followed her lead in a teasing mood. ''Though I confess I do find those fish scales somewhat disagreeable after a time.''

The lighthearted banter continued as they made their circuit around the park, but for once it was a strain for Lord Nicholas. He was upset with himself that he had allowed Lady Brad to pierce, in however small a way, his protective shell. Some things he kept very private, most especially anything to do with his family. That the Duke of Chance heartily despised both his sons was no secret. That Lord Nicholas was not the most devoted of sons was consequently supposed. But whether Devlin felt any emotion deeper than annoyance over the family divisions was utterly secret. Even Lord Ronald, who also suffered from parental ire, did not guess the emotions disguised by that heavy-lidded gaze.

His slight distraction served him badly when he returned Lady Bradamant to Lady Bellingham's care. He stopped to chat for a while—the ring was duly admired—but he was anxious to get away by

himself for a time, and it showed. And was noticed
by the ladies. Finally they allowed him to escape, but
only after extracting the promise of his escort to a
large number of upcoming events. They were already engaged for a rout party that very evening. He
was not to be let off the leash, merely permitted a
longer rein.

Devlin was greatly troubled in mind over his inability to comprehend his enthusiastic fiancée. It is
extremely doubtful whether he would have been in
any way comforted by closer acquaintance with her
mental processes.

Certainly Lady Bellingham, who was in Lady
Brad's confidence, was nearly as troubled as the disturbed Don Juan. That poor lady was once again
being subjected to her companion's imitation of the
caged lions at the Royal Exchange, only somehow
Lady Brad seemed far more dangerous as she proceeded to wear out the carpet in Lady Bellingham's
private sitting room.

"Did you see?" she demanded rhetorically as she
went on immediately to answer her own question.
"Of course you did. You could not help but see him
squirm! My God, but he's frightened! Now, are you
going to try to tell me again that he sincerely meant
to propose, that he wants to marry me?"

Lady Bellingham had, of course, noticed Lord
Nicholas's strange hesitancy, had even been sparked
to a brief moment of spite the other morning, but she
was essentially a gentle soul who hated to think ill of

anyone. "Well, my dear, you know, even the best of men—yes, as even my own darling Lord B. did—may experience a moment of fear, of panic, when he is about to give up his freedom, however much in love he may be, and however much he truly wishes to marry," she said trying to excuse the frightened fiancé.

"Fear? He was petrified! You should have seen him at the church. Napoleon's Grande Armée could not have scared him more than one clergyman!"

"Oh? With George it was writing out invitations," she offered in a reminiscent tone.

"Did Lord Bellingham take care to remind you of all the disadvantages to your marriage as well? Threaten you with poverty, isolation? Continue to flirt with other women before your very eyes?" This was hardly a fair question. The late earl had been extremely wealthy and sociable, and although he had been the light of his dear lady's eyes, had been precluded from being taken seriously as a flirt by a short, rather rotund form and a shiny, balding pate, even when he was relatively young.

"Did Lord Nicholas flirt, dear?" Lady Bellingham countered with another question.

"With every woman in sight, and during the Grand Strut that's more than a few! He even publicly acknowledged Harriet Wilson! Even Little Harry was shocked at that."

"I should think so!" The ladies of society knew very well who Harriet Wilson was, what she did and generally with whom she did it, but they pretended not to, and the gentlemen encouraged the pretense. So, while the gentlemen privately patronized courtesans like Little Harry, in public they denied the existence of such women. Lady Bellingham was shocked in spite of herself.

Outrage sat oddly on her amiable countenance. Lady Brad, seeing her expression, was finally stopped in her tracks. She gave a delightful peal of laughter and leaned over the chair where her friend sat.

"Tell me, dear heart, if you truly believe Devlin to be merely suffering from a momentary agitation of the nerves, why did you set a date for the wedding?"

"I don't know," Lady Bellingham wailed in protest. "And I wish I had not—I have not been able to sleep a wink since."

"You know very well why you did it," said Lady Brad, tenaciously keeping to the point. "You realized he was trying to discourage me to the point of calling the whole thing off, and were quite properly offended. Only you cannot bear to think badly of anyone, so you keep trying to find excuses for his reprehensible conduct, when, in fact, there are none."

"And what excuse is there for your conduct?" The older woman attacked in self-defense. "I want you to drop this silly scheme entirely! It frightens me.

Something is going to go wrong. I can feel it! Hasn't he been punished enough already?'' she pleaded.

"No, he has not even begun to suffer." Lady Brad was unmerciful.

DEVLIN HAD INDEED BEGUN to suffer. Besides the discomfort of an undesirable and frighteningly tenacious fiancée, Lord Nicholas discovered in that maddening lady an amazing and most annoying talent for reminding him of what few noble sentiments remained to him. She had looked at him with that distressingly direct gaze and said that she believed him capable of good. She continually, by word and action, challenged him to look at himself and his rakish behavior, and it tended to look excessively silly, if not worse.

Most of all, she reminded him of Charlie, which he considered very odd, for they were not in the least alike. Unless, assuming Ronnie was correct, they both truly cared for him. Charlie was the only thing in Devlin's life that saved him from being a complete cynic. Because of Charlie, he had known love, a deep, unspoken fraternal tie, and had seen love—the love between Charlie and his wife. Charlie's Ann also served to remind him that it was possible, if extremely rare, for a woman to be honest, real, capable of deep and true affection. He thought sometimes that Lady Brad might be that kind of woman, if it were not for his continuing suspicion that she was not being honest with him.

Despite his best intentions he found, too, that it was far from easy to maintain his usual composure in Lady Brad's presence. He was rattled, and as a result his first endeavors to break with her were somewhat clumsy.

In his attempt to flirt with every woman in sight, Lord Nick allowed himself to be dragged to any number of evening parties that he would otherwise have steadfastly avoided, and though nominally in attendance upon his fiancée, he managed to spread his favors remarkably well.

The ploy was too great a departure from custom to succeed. Instead, Devlin's behavior was taken as proof of his devotion and a belated recognition of his social responsibilities. Even his old flirts ceased to take him seriously. The pose of constant attendance once assumed proved difficult to drop. Unable to escape to the gaming tables at White's, Devlin tried first to gravitate away from the dance floor to the card tables at the various assemblies they attended. Lady Brad let him go, but not alone. With her cool gray eyes watching his every move, Nick could hardly make a credible showing as a profligate gambler. What if Brad caught him cheating so as to lose?

He next tried wagers. Lady Brad made them appear a private jest. He tried showy and reckless expense, within careful limits. A letter from the Reverend Jonathan Fenster, revealing the desperate state of affairs at Devlin's Yorkshire estate, provided a genuine threat of poverty—all to no avail.

Faced with a life of deprivation and isolation, Lady Brad showed concern only for Devlin's tenants. And that funny look was back in her eye—the one that gave his conscience uncomfortable twinges. The distressing notion occurred to Lord Nick that even with his freedom regained, his life would never be the same again.

WHILE LORD NICHOLAS tried subtly to convince Lady Bradamant of his ineligibility as a husband, Lady Bellingham was trying openly and most vocally to end the relationship as well.

"I feel trouble," she proclaimed for about the hundredth time. "I have the same feeling, here—" she clutched a generous bosom in a manner worthy of Mrs. Siddons "—as I did when the aunt who was supposed to sponsor my season eloped with her second footman, and my come-out had to be postponed until the scandal blew over. And the time that very distinguished military gentleman tried to sell George shares in an Indian trading company that was discovered not to exist except in his imagination. George—" she nodded wisely "—listened to me."

"Lord Bellingham, by all accounts, was so besotted that had he known of the fraud and you told him to buy, he'd have done it," Lady Brad retorted affectionately.

"Yes," Lady Bellingham recalled, "George was a darling, the perfect spouse. And," she continued, not successfully distracted, "somewhere, I hope, there may be a husband just as dear and loving waiting for you. But you won't find him while you are engaged to another man, or when you are excluded from polite society after causing the most dreadful scandal! Nor will you find happiness dedicating your life to the punishment of deceitful rakes!''

"Kate, dear, you worry too much.''

"Worry? Of course I worry. I cannot even decide which is worse—jilting the man or marrying him. Yes, I can. You must promise not to marry him, dear. He would probably behave so outrageously you would have to leave him eventually, so it would be much better to get it over with now. The closer we get to the wedding day, the more scandalous it will be.''

"The wedding date you set,'' Brad reminded her, unrepentant.

"Oh, don't remind me, you dreadful girl. You know why I did it. I was angry. I will even admit that you were perfectly correct about Lord Nicholas's behavior. But just because Devlin is a wicked seducer is no excuse for you to wreck your future over the bounder.''

"I have no intention of ruining my future, my love, only of ensuring that Lord Nick does not ruin the future of any female ever again.''

This sounded frighteningly to Lady Bellingham as if the girl actually meant to keep the rogue, for she doubted if Devlin could be controlled except by constant surveillance, and perhaps not even then.

"Brad, what was the purpose of having a season in town?"

"To get myself a husband," Lady Brad agreed amicably.

"Now, don't tell me you've got one. I refuse to believe you mean to go through with it. So you jilt him. And then what?"

"I had hoped that you would still desire me to stay as your companion," she answered gently. "Unless, of course, you mean to throw me out?"

This teasing suggestion was answered by an outbreak of tears.

"Katy, sweetie, don't cry." Lady Brad provided a handkerchief and a comforting shoulder. "I shall be very much offended if the thought of my presence is so dismaying as to drive you to tears."

"Oh, don't be silly," the widowed countess replied, sobbing. "You know I love you. I could not love you any better if you were my very own. And if you were my very own, I'd...I'd lock you up and starve you on bread and water before I let you throw your life away like this."

"Now, now, how many times must I tell you? I am not throwing my life away."

"You are if you end up dwindling into an old maid companion to a cranky old lady, always at somebody's beck and call, with never a life of your own."

"You mean a husband of my own. So instead of being at your beck and call, I could be at the beck and call of some demanding gentleman."

"The right gentleman, I hope. I won't tell you, as most society mamas would, that any marriage is better than none. You have the strength to make your own way if you have to, as you had to do in the past. But you need not fend for yourself. There is so much love in you, Brad, darling. I cannot believe that there is not a man worthy of that love somewhere."

"Why, I would like to think so, too, Katy. But he is not likely to appear on command. And he certainly is not in London this season. I have looked at all the prospects, and there are only one or two young men I could even be friends with, let alone entertain warmer feelings for. I tell you what—you have my solemn promise that if a likely gentleman comes along I will dispose of milord Nicholas Devlin so quickly his head will reel."

With this, Lady Bellingham had, perforce, to be satisfied. But she prayed devoutly for a man who could captivate Bradamant and turn her from her avowed purpose.

Lord Nicholas went further than praying. He proceeded to throw eligible bachelors before his fiancée as one might strew rose petals. Even he was not surprised when his efforts were unsuccessful, as he explained to Lord Ronald Graham.

"Well, of course, she wasn't interested. I have noticed she gives them all a little test, just to see if they can follow her conversation, if they have the slightest sense of humor. For some strange reason the only

ones who pass the test are all as bad as I, or worse—
fortune hunters and rakes every one. And she hasn't
enough money to lure the fortune hunters past mild
flirtation.''

"What about Lord Arun? Did you try him? Very
intelligent is Arun.''

"Very intellectual, you mean. He'd bury her in the
British Museum. Lady Brad deserves better than
that.''

"She deserves better than you,'' Lord Ronald reminded him. "And the British Museum is better than
Yorkshire.''

"Very true,'' Devlin agreed. "Well, I can try him,
but I don't expect any luck. I think I will have to
move quickly and find something on which we can
disagree—violently and irrevocably.''

CHAPTER FIVE

"DARLING, MUST WE GO to the Asterleys'? It seems I never see you anymore, unless surrounded by the *haut ton*. And you promised the wedding preparations would not come between us." The languorous, heavy-lidded look was back.

"Did you have something in mind, Nick?" Lady Bradamant managed a creditable imitation of his sensuous gaze.

"Yes. Now, don't laugh. I have given this considerable thought, and the only way we can escape our chaperons is . . . to go sight-seeing."

"Sight-seeing?" She laughed, genuinely surprised.

"Yes, of course. We won't be surrounded by well-wishers. Lady Bellingham's feet won't hold up—yes, I love the darling, too, but she is not the girl I am going to marry." *And neither are you,* he said to himself, *if I can do anything to prevent it.* "If I know anything about women, and I do," he admitted with a wicked gleam, "your companion will be perfectly happy to wait quietly on a comfortable bench while we wear ourselves out."

"My feet won't give out," she promised rashly. "Where do we start?"

"I thought the Tower of London."

Oddly enough, Lord Nicholas enjoyed the Tower, which he had not visited since his brother had taken him as a child. He and Lady Brad laughed over the pompous perorations of the guidebook he had purchased. Brad was really interested in history, too, not just sentimental about old legends, told inaccurately. The execution of Ann Boleyn, related in gory detail by one of the attendants, was greeted with the grumbled aside, "Served her right."

While they argued over the questionable virtues of the Tudor monarchs—"My dear Nick, had you spent any time in Yorkshire, you would know Richard the Third was by far the better man"—Devlin searched for a subject for a real quarrel. What he slowly came to realize, however, was how much they thought alike. They never had to explain their jokes to each other. Time after time, when something amusing happened, he would catch her eyes and see the laughter there.

The difficulty was that he was known to be liberal. Had he been able to claim belief in slavery, or oppression of the lower classes, Brad would have been truly horrified. This was, unfortunately, too much out of character to seem in the least likely. Indeed, the words stuck in Nick's throat. When he should have been agreeing to the usefulness of women and children working in the new factories, he got angry and gave a lecture on unsafe conditions and slave wages. And he could not regret the outburst, even though it caused Brad to look at him with warm, admiring eyes. For the first time he honestly thought she liked him.

While walking through Westminster Abbey he tried another tack. "I don't believe in this, of course. All this glory to honor a nonexistent God." *There, that should give her a shock,* he thought.

"Oh, are you an atheist? I am so sorry." Lady Brad acted as if he had just excused himself from an invitation because of a minor indisposition.

Nick was annoyed. "There is no need to feel sorry for me."

"No, of course, dear," she agreed politely, as if to quiet an unruly child. "It is very generous of you to agree to a church wedding, believing as you do."

"Oh, that's all right," he conceded somewhat grudgingly. "But," he tried again with renewed hope and zeal, "of course, I won't have our children's wits befuddled by any religious nonsense."

"I expect they will make up their own minds. People, even children, generally do. But I don't see how we can hide the fact that others—other people—do believe in God. And children so hate being different."

Devlin took a deep breath. Better to get Lady Brad to make a statement with which he could disagree. With an arm tucked confidingly around her waist, he asked, "Have you given any thought to how many children you would like to have?"

"As many as we do have," she responded calmly and cleverly.

Well, since he had already decided on the mythical family's upbringing, he could not claim to want none. So he tried the other extreme. "I'd like lots, a round dozen. Charlie has six."

There—she was giving him that look again. "Yes, you will make a good father." Brad gave him a minute to regain his composure. "Have you ever seen your brother's children?"

"No, no, they were all born in India. We may have the opportunity soon, though. Lucien claims Charlie means to send the older ones over here for some town bronze. Charlie—his eldest son I mean—will be eighteen, and Nicky—the next is named after me—" he revealed with self-conscious pride, "is only a year behind."

"Will they stay with the duke?" Brad asked in all innocence.

"No!" The answer was unnecessarily forceful. "That may be what the Duke of Chance and Sir Lucien Rendall expect, but that is something Charlie would never do, not in a million years."

Devlin retreated into a moody silence that had nothing to do with the ugliness of the abbey's effigies. When he spoke it was in a spirit of grim determination.

"You know, Brad, darling, I have been very remiss in not making you known to my family. The duke rarely travels to the metropolis, preferring to hold court at Chance. I must arrange a long visit, so you can get to know each other. Yes, you must be introduced to the duke."

CHAPTER SIX

"DAMN THE WOMAN! I have never known anyone so difficult to quarrel with! Do you realize I even claimed I was an atheist, and she did not so much as blink?"

Lord Ronald, astonished, swallowed his punch in a sudden gulp. "You never said such a thing!"

"And that I wanted the children brought up that way—all twelve of them."

"What did she say to that?"

"She said she believed I would be a very good father."

"Good God."

"Exactly. Now what can I say to shock a woman like that? The trouble is, Brad's different, not one of those prim mealymouthed schoolgirls who haven't a thought that Mama has not sanctioned. Brad isn't shocked or offended by original thought; she revels in it. The only thing that would disgust her would be if I turned into a...a mindless, malicious fop like my cousin Lucien. I doubt the transformation would be credible."

They cogitated, assisted by more punch.

"She's a spirited thing," Lord Ronald said at last. "Have you tried to give any orders? Correct her behavior?"

"Oh, that really would be rich—the Devil telling her how to behave. Besides, what is there to correct?"

"Say she flirts too much. Be jealous."

"How much will you wager she laps it up? I would much rather she did not trust me than seem overly devoted."

"Then you should not spend so much time alone together," Lord Ronald pointed out. "Alvanley saw you with her at Hampton Court—looking very cozy, he said, and no chaperon in sight. Now everybody's talking about what an unfashionably affectionate couple you are."

"Damn! I can't help that. She makes me laugh sometimes. I don't know what to do anymore. I've written to my revered sire, and I'm taking her to Chance, hoping for a miracle. If the old man thinks I really want this marriage, as society does now, he will assuredly try to destroy the match. Perhaps, just once, he will do something for his son—all unaware."

Lord Ronald had ignored this last speech, having been possessed by a magnificent thought. "Nick, Nick, I've got it!" He shook the brooding man's shoulder, accidentally spilling punch over his breeches.

"Well, you needn't douse me to attract attention. What have you got, clunch?"

"For all her liberal views, Lady Brad is a very properly behaved young lady, isn't that so?"

"Well, of course she is," Lord Nick replied impatiently and somewhat huffily at the implied slur to her reputation.

"Nick, have you ever kissed her? I mean, *really* kissed her?"

Startled, Devlin looked at his friend with real admiration. "No, no, I have not. Ronnie, I think you have got something! I have been much too well-behaved, almost reverent. It's about time a little passion entered out relationship. If she loves me, truly loves me, she won't hold me off." Lord Nick delivered the seducer's standard patter with a wicked flash in his eyes. For the first time in weeks he saw hope. The gentlemen laughed merrily, quite forgetting, of course, the old saw that he laughs best who laughs last.

Vauxhall Gardens was the setting the experienced rake chose for his sham seduction. Lady Bellingham was not entirely happy about the excursion. The Gardens were no longer so exclusive in clientele as she would wish; indeed, there was now a distinctly rowdy, vulgar element, better to be avoided by people of taste and discrimination. It was no longer safe to walk in some parts. But Brad wanted very much to hear the new soprano who was to perform there, and one could hardly doubt Devlin's ability to pro-

tect a score of ladies. An old beau of Lady Bellingham's provided extra support as well, and flirted so
successfully that she was unlikely to notice anyone
else's improper behavior. To emphasize their re-
spectability she had taken the precaution of dressing
in her primmest gown, very much the dowager, and
had insisted Brad do the same, adding a lace fichu to
an already innocent gown of white muslin.

The soprano was good, the wafer-thin ham slices
justly famous and the champagne excellent. Devlin
had not the least difficulty in removing his fiancée
from their box for the gentle stroll.

With her mind still on the music, Bradamant
barely noticed when their walk reached the more se-
cluded and poorly lit parts of the Gardens, and her
escort's attentions began to grow increasingly warm.
When, embracing her lightly, Devlin began to nib-
ble on her ear, Lady Brad did suffer a moment's
shock. She stiffened in his embrace, to his great delight.

Nick had long since ceased to expect any kind of
perception from his flirts, with good reason. It was
very difficult to exercise one's mental faculties when
being made love to by an acknowledged expert. But,
as Devlin had already learned to his cost, Brad was
different. She had made a particular study of Lord
Nicholas Devlin and therefore recognized that slight
momentary expression of pleasure for what it was—
triumph. Before Devlin could resume his embrace
she threw her arms about his neck, leaned seduc-

tively against the seducer and pressed her lips to his, hoping briefly in her inexperience that she was doing it properly.

It was the last thought either of them was to have for some time. Motivations were completely forgotten as the kiss continued and deepened. Bradamant found the correct response to his lovemaking seemed to come very naturally, despite her innocence. She was not in the least surprised when the kiss became amazingly intimate and his hands wandered in soft caresses.

They were finally awakened from their reverie by a group of drunken roisterers. Nick hid her from view as they passed by. Brad was still leaning weakly against his chest as he tried to regain his breath. The hand that smoothed her soft curls trembled slightly.

Both were quiet for the remainder of the evening, returning back to the box and then home in the carriage, but it was not an uncomfortable or embarrassed silence. Nick had, after all, managed to shock his fiancée, but he had shocked himself even more.

LORD RONALD did not understand why his query as to how the false seduction had gone was rather rudely put off. Devlin was still trying to analyze within himself the strange sensations of that evening.

It was not merely that he had suddenly been most forcibly reminded that Lady Bradamant Mount-Aubin was extremely desirable. Devlin had known, intimately, any number of desirable women, none of whom had affected him as Bradamant had. For the first time in his experiences, he had lost control of the situation. Heaven only knows what would have happened had they not been interrupted, for he was quite oblivious to where they were. He might not have stopped, and Brad obviously was not about to box his ears in outraged innocence. Now he dared not press further. Brad could not be depended upon to refuse, outraged or not. Considering the circumstances, should he successfully seduce his fiancée he would truly feel obliged to marry her after all.

He was becoming resigned to the idea of their marriage anyway, since he could see no rescue in sight. Or, at least, he believed the emotion to be resignation. They had been engaged now for two months, and he had accustomed himself to the prospect. So he thought. When a letter from his brother indicated he intended to relocate his family in England, Nick did not even think to pull this forward as an excuse to delay the wedding, although he wished Charlie could be present. Had Charlie been there he could have told Nicholas that when a man finds one girl so totally different from all others it means only one thing.

Lady Bradamant was equally disturbed by their encounter. She tried to discount her reaction by dwelling on her own innocence and Devlin's legendary expertise, but she was not entirely successful.

What was even worse than this remembered passion, however, was Devlin's subsequent behavior. Brad's zeal for vengeance was easy to maintain when he squirmed and sought means of escape, but it looked as if he had given up the fight. Despite Lady Bellingham's worries, Brad had never intended to go through with the wedding. She meant to give Lord Nick the fright of his life, and then, when he was consumed in panic, send him off with a flea in his ear. Devlin no longer seemed unduly upset at the idea of married life immured in the wilds of Yorkshire. He discussed arrangements for the wedding and breakfast without a flicker of dismay. His claim to have made the plans for their removal to Yorkshire proved, upon examination, to be quite true.

And Lady Bradamant discovered once again how perversely likable the man was. She had always liked him—that was why she had been so upset at his dastardly behavior in the first place. It would be very easy, she realized, to forget the engagement was not genuine. Lady Bellingham's gloomy prognostications came often to mind, although Kate, too, had ceased to complain. Devlin's meek attitude had thrown her plans for vengeance into turmoil, and indeed, when they were together revenge was far from her mind.

Meanwhile, the engaged pair, accompanied by Lady Bellingham, set out for Chance, principal seat of the Devlin family since the sixteenth century. As one might expect, the family fortunes had originally been made by an Elizabethan pirate who, in addition to plundering Spanish ships, knew well how to make himself agreeable to the ladies, more especially the queen. In the coach Lord Nick amused his betrothed with tales of the family chronicles, only slightly exaggerated, while their chaperon dozed in the corner. Despite his attempt to appear cheerful, Brad could see that every mile that brought them closer to Chance increased some internal agitation in Lord Nick.

She had realized that Devlin was not on good terms with his father, suspected the duke to be...unamiable. After all, something must have been badly wrong to send Nick running off to sea when he was but a youth and his brother all the way to India as soon as he reached his majority. Still, she took courage in hand and asked, "Who will be in residence besides your...the duke, Nick?" She had also noticed that Nick never referred to his surviving parent as "father."

"Let me see. There are probably a few maiden aunts, whom you won't be able to tell apart, so you need not really try. There was a sycophantic chaplain in my day, an equally sycophantic secretary—the duke is trying to clean up the family history, a task so difficult he has been working on it these past thirty years. Sir Lucien Rendall, a distant relative but, alas, not distant enough, is thankfully out of the country, or we would have to endure his presence. Having no fortune of his own, he finds it convenient to batten on the duke most of the year. We will, however, have to deal with his mama. Lady Rendall has never recovered from the injustice of having her son deprived of the dukedom by eight utterly unworthy and undeserving closer male relatives. The duke tends to agree with her. I call her aunt, but she is, thank God, nothing of the kind. There may be any number of other hangers-on as well, but they all tend to blend in with one another. There is only one point of view at Chance, and that is the duke's. His grace does not encourage individuality in his dependents.''

"How dull it sounds! I hope you won't be too bored.'' Actually, it sounded perfectly awful, and Brad was considering stopping the coach.

They were entering the heavy wrought-iron gates now, so it was too late. Nick looked as if he, too, would have liked to escape. "It won't be dull,'' he promised in a low voice. It was a warning, and his eyes were bleak as he uttered it.

Brad squeezed his hand comfortingly as they went to beard the dragon in his lair.

At first glance the ducal manor seemed grim enough to figure in any of Mrs. Radcliffe's romances, but appearances were deceptive. An overabundance of thick, dark foliage gave Chance its shadowy, menacing aspect. But the manor house itself had been continually altered in shape by succeeding generations with no attempt to adapt to previous styles, so that a cheerfully tasteless and vulgar monstrosity now loomed before them. If Brad had not been so nervous, the sight would have made her laugh.

Devlin's predictions were perfectly correct. The numerous inhabitants of the estate were permitted only a vague, shadowy existence as extensions of the duke's will, but Lady Rendall, acting as his hostess, stood out from the rest by virtue of sheer malice. The others merely reflected the duke's hatred of his son; she hated him for her own sake. Such was their welcome to Chance.

"So this is the young . . . woman you have chosen to honor with the name of Devlin? I am surprised, Nicholas. She quite looks like a lady," the duke greeted them in a deliberately insulting tone. Naturally, he had taken it for granted that only the lowest type of female would accept his son.

Lady Bellingham sputtered and looked as if, for once in her timid life, she might resort to violence. She might have been forestalled by Lord Nicholas in this intent if Brad had not halted them all in surprise by a delighted peal of laughter.

"I am disappointed in you, your grace. My father told me so much of your reputed omniscience and power that I felt quite sure you would have had my background investigated long since."

"Your father?"

"The late Earl of Hampton. I believe you were slightly acquainted?" Brad regarded the duke without fear. His eyes and voice spoke of power, but she noticed that his lips had a blue tinge she remembered seeing on her father, and he leaned heavily on his cane.

"We were," he answered coldly. The Earl of Hampton might have left his daughter poorly provided in worldly goods, but he left her a heritage much older and more respectable than that of the Devlins.

Round one to Lady Bradamant Mount-Aubin.

THROUGHOUT THE NEXT few days the duke, ably assisted by Lady Rendall, tried to discover faults in Devlin's fiancée, while continually denigrating Lord Nick's own worthiness. At last only one fault could be justly imputed to her—lack of fortune. It was a fault the duke rather liked.

During the daily torture known as dinner, always conducted with the greatest formality in a dining hall that could easily have accommodated the entire House of Lords, the duke began another ploy. Lady Bradamant, seated at his side during the meal, listened as he described to her how much more comfort she might enjoy, could she persuade her husband-to-be to return to the family home. Obviously Chance was quite large enough to enable them to live in complete comfort and grant them sufficient privacy. Nick, who could overhear but by the conventions of society was not supposed to enter into conversation so far down the table, choked in anger and nearly rose from his seat, until he caught a sign from Bradamant. To all the duke's persuasions she merely answered that she and Nick would be quite comfortable in Yorkshire. When he announced that his grandsons would be visiting soon, Brad merely raised an elegant eyebrow and said, "Really?" in a manner copied from Brummell. Nick could have applauded.

Later, when the gentlemen had rejoined the ladies for tea in the drawing room, Devlin looked more than merely harassed. Afraid of an explosion, Brad hoped to distract her fiancé by leading him out onto the terrace.

He followed her as she disappeared into the formal gardens; then he marched her in silence to a maze set within. Brad wondered for a while if he had forgotten her presence, but he finally burst out, "Well, Brad, now that you have seen what kind of family I have, are you sure you want to ally yourself with me?"

This was not part of his scheme, as had been those earlier efforts to break their engagement. This was a cry of deep torment, and Brad knew it.

"Every family has a few black sheep, Nick. I must admit yours seems to have more than their share, but—" she pulled on his hand for attention "—you are not like them. Nor is your brother, from what I gather."

"No, Charlie's all right. But, God, to think I share the same blood as that monster! I swore I would not let him upset me, but he is incorrigible, horrible! You do not know how horrible." In his anguish he had completely missed the imputation that the duke, and not the notorious Nick, was the family black sheep.

She guided him to a marble bench. ''Tell me.'' Perhaps this would help her understand the enigma of Lord Nicholas.

''I never knew my mother. Trying to satisfy his standards destroyed her—literally. She was told, after Charlie was born, that another pregnancy would be dangerous. But the duke wanted a second son, just in case. She grew weaker with each miscarriage, until she finally died giving birth to me. He didn't care. He didn't care about me, either, as long as Charlie was there—which was fine with me.

''For eleven years I watched him try to force Charlie into his idea of what a Devlin should be, and Charlie just could not be what he wanted. Chance wanted him to be the best...and Charlie was just average in all the things he was supposed to succeed in. Charlie is kind and warmhearted, but the duke wanted him to be as stiff-necked as he is. Charlie just put up with it all—until he was told who had been chosen for his bride.

''The whole neighborhood, Chance included, knew Charlie and Ann were in love, were made for each other. But Ann's family wasn't good enough. I was so happy when he told me they were going to elope. I helped make sure he got away.

''Well, from that day the Marquis of Welting ceased to exist for Chance. I think he believed Charlie would die, and considering the conditions in the

East, I suppose it might have been likely. Suddenly my existence was recognized and he tried to remake me instead. Except that I fought, so I was more heavily punished. When I heard, at age sixteen, that he meant to pass my brother's ex-fiancée to me, I bolted. But he's never given up. He never will. He has this . . . compulsion to control.''

"He cannot control us, Nick. He has nothing we want."

"No, but that doesn't make his efforts any less monstrous. Don't you find him frightening, disgusting?"

"I find him pathetic." She had shocked Nick into listening. "I told you—he is powerless to touch us. And he's old, Nick. No, not just old, he's dying—and he knows it. I suspect your brother realizes it, too, and that is why he's coming home. It won't be long now. Charlie will be the Duke of Chance, and this building, which seems so grim now, will be free of all those parasites. Instead, the halls will echo with the boyish high spirits of young Charlie, Nicky and all the rest."

Finally he smiled. "George, Theo, Joe and baby Bertie," he completed for her.

As if it were the most natural thing in the world, as perhaps it was, Brad welcomed Nick into her arms.

"You're so good for me, Brad," he murmured into her hair. "I keep thinking, if you care for me I can't be so worthless after all."

The embrace had been meant to give comfort and solace, but suddenly it was Vauxhall all over again. This time they were interrupted by Mother Nature, who opened the heavens in a torrent of rain.

Nick knew of a side entrance so they could avoid the disapproving looks of the Devlin clan. Running up the marble stairs to their chambers, they laughed like children. Outside Brad's room Nick suddenly grabbed and kissed her again, leaving her more than a little bemused later as she changed out of her wet clothes.

Devlin's eyes, however, were finally open. The libertine had met his match. Lord Nicholas had fallen madly in love with his own fiancée.

BASKING IN THIS NEW KNOWLEDGE, all Devlin longed for was time alone with his beloved. In this he was to be foiled, although not, as he expected, by his unamiable sire. The very next morning brought a surprise visitor in the person of the Reverend Jonathan Fenster.

The vicar was a mild-mannered gentleman of about sixty years, who was much in awe of his ducal surroundings, but not so much in awe as to be put off. However, Lord Nicholas made him wait until Lady Bradamant could join them. She would know what to do.

"Darling, this is the Reverend Mr. Fenster. He's come to tell us how things stand at home. Sir, this is my betrothed, Lady Bradamant Mount-Aubin."

"Good morning, Vicar. Dear me, the situation must be very bad indeed to send you chasing after Lord Nicholas." She invited him to sit in one of the straight-backed Carolinian chairs that the duke provided for his guests' discomfort.

"Yes, my lady. I'm afraid the situation is truly desperate. But not without hope, and that is why I have come, er, chasing after Lord Nicholas."

"Has something happened since you wrote your letter?" Nick asked.

"Harcourt, the bailiff, you know, has discovered you mean to marry. He realizes that eventually attention will be brought to his own misdeeds, and he means to clear out with everything he can lay his hands on. In his hurry he is being less than careful."

"He has no idea we've been corresponding?"

"None. And while he might suspect me of interfering, he believes me to be convalescing from influenza in the Lake District at present."

"But he must be meaning to disappear very shortly," Lady Brad interjected.

"Yes," the reverend gentleman agreed. "I believe he thinks himself safe until the wedding. But that means we must move before that."

"We could both go," Nick pleaded, reaching for his fiancée's hand.

"No, darling," she refused him regretfully. "You know it would only make him suspicious. In fact, any stranger at this point might look odd in such an isolated community. I was trying to think of some disguise for you."

The vicar blushed modestly. "I rather think, my lady, that I can provide such a disguise. At present my parish is being attended to by a neighboring clergyman, but it has been suggested, especially since my recent bout of ill health, and considering my advanced age, that I could usefully employ the services of a young curate."

The suggestion was greeted, not unkindly, by hoots of laughter from Lady Brad. "How delicious! Nick a curate? Oh, I only wish I might see it!"

"Do you doubt my acting ability?" Devlin lifted his brows haughtily in mock offense.

"Haven't I said so before? You can do anything."

"I shall stoop and wear spectacles," Nick decided.

"And you must leave at once," the vicar added.

"Damn!—I'm sorry, Vicar—I suppose I must. I hate to leave you." This last was directed to his beloved.

"Yes, I know, Nick. But the sooner you leave, the sooner you can return. And while you are there you can take inventory of what bare necessities we shall have to bring from London. It would be comforting to know that at least a few of the rooms are habitable."

"I think I can assure you that the basic fabric of the house is perfectly sound," the vicar informed her dryly. "Mr. Harcourt has seen fit to inhabit the manor for the last five years."

"Come, Vicar, I'll see you settled here for to-night. No, no trouble at all. We can set out for Yorkshire early tomorrow."

"And Lady Bellingham and I," Brad announced to Nick later, "can set off for London. Thank heaven, we now have an excuse to cut short our visit. London society never looked so attractive."

"I shall miss you," he whispered into her ear.

"Nonsense. You will enjoy yourself immensely. You will be far too busy masquerading and foiling criminals to have time to miss me."

"I will still miss you."

At moments like these Lord Nick forgot that he had ever questioned Lady Brad's motives for accepting his suit. When he kissed her he was likely to forget why he had first proposed. Unfortunately, others remembered.

CHAPTER SEVEN

LADY BELLINGHAM CONTINUED to have palpitations, a sure omen of disaster, but refrained from trying to reason with her companion, considering it quite useless. Although she did her best to hide it, Lady Bradamant was also uneasy in her mind. The wedding day was only weeks away now. All the preparations had been made exactly as if the ceremony were going to take place, although the gala party had been canceled because the exact date of Devlin's return was uncertain. A trousseau had been selected and flowers ordered for the church, ices for the reception. Gifts were pouring in from friends and relations—Devlin's friends as well as hers. These Bradamant steadfastly refused to open or send back—yet. One even appeared from the present Earl of Hampton, but it was returned immediately. Although the invitations had all been sent, the earl and his family did not receive one.

Which hardly matters, as there is to be no wedding, Lady Brad told herself. Nick had never really meant to propose, had tried desperately to free himself, and she had only meant to make him suffer for trying to seduce a virtuous woman. Therefore, they had never really been engaged at all, she reasoned. The only trouble was that she did not want revenge against Nick anymore; she wanted to marry him.

And she no longer knew for sure what Nick wanted. Worse, he was two hundred miles away. Oh, he wrote faithfully every day, just as he had promised: silly, passionate notes saying how he longed to make love to her (was he trying to shock her again?); businesslike reports on the poor condition of the land; boasting descriptions of his investigations disguised as the meek curate, and always solemn oaths to return in time for the wedding. But Bradamant never felt secure unless she could see his expression, and even then he was too expert at deception.

She had always known that Devlin would marry her if she forced him. Her entire scheme of vengeance was based on that fact. And finally, it seemed that he had resigned himself to the marriage, resolved to make the best of it. Nick would be generous enough to admit that he had brought it on himself.

But was it not possible that, like Bradamant, Nick had come to feel a deeper affection and might actually like to marry her? Perhaps he would even prefer to go through with it rather than deal with the embarrassment attendant upon being jilted? For he would certainly be blamed. No one really believed that Lord Nicholas Devlin, survivor of a dozen duels, seducer of more women than the legendary Don Juan, gamester, fortune hunter and in general, a ne'er-do-well, could reform. The question was, was society right, or was she?

There was only one thing to do. Nick would be offered his freedom, but not in the terms Brad had originally intended. He would refuse, of course, but Brad knew him well enough to see if he truly meant it. A fleeting look of hope or relief, a pause before a too-insistent denial, and it would be over.

But how long would she have to wait?

DEVLIN, ALL UNAWARE of the turmoil he had aroused in his beloved, was subject to a false sense of security. He had not heard of Lady Bellingham's famous palpitations.

Once he had disposed of the rascal Harcourt—caught red-handed trying to strip the manor of furnishings—he set himself to making a home ready for his bride. Parts of the house were in excellent condition, for Harcourt had kept it up for himself, but it lacked a feminine touch. New servants had to be hired, with the greatly appreciated help of the vicar, for Nick would have nothing to do with the bailiff's hangers-on. To surprise Bradamant he had a private sitting room prepared for her, taking care to choose colors and fabrics to her taste. The master bedroom suite was redone as well, to fumigate it of the bailiff's presence.

He missed Bradamant. It needed this separation to show him how accustomed he had become to their close communion, to her swift appreciation of the absurd. She responded to his letters, but he found these missives less than revealing. Indeed, the only times he had felt at all sure of her affection was when they had shared laughter, or an embrace.

The vicar promised to see that all the work was completed on time, both in the house and out in the grounds. The Reverend Fenster had been very impressed by the future Lady Nicholas.

Two weeks before the wedding, Lord Nick set forth to return to his betrothed's waiting arms, full of joy and hope. He did not know that his nemesis would be waiting with her—in the unexpected form of Lord Ronald Graham.

LORD RONALD WAS WORRIED about his friend. Nick was in a terrible spot—and he felt partially to blame. Nick had been trying to do a kindness for him when he got caught in this dreadful trap. Ronnie knew himself to have been very green when he first came to town. Without Nick's subtle guidance he would have dropped into any number of pitfalls for the unwary. After all Nick's kindness and advice, Ronnie felt there ought to be something he could do in return to help Nick out.

And now even Devlin had given up! He had written Lord Ronald from Yorkshire requesting him to be best man. Oh, he had tried to sound cheerful, but Ronnie knew better. How could anyone become resigned to such a fate? Impossible! Marriage alone was bad enough, but to be tied to a bluestocking past her first youth, without great beauty or fortune, was not to be thought of.

Lord Ronald brooded alone, as he could not admit anyone to Nick's dread secret. He reviewed in his befuddled mind all the solutions he and Nick had discussed. The threat of poverty had not worked, nor the fear of infidelity. Lady Bradamant had faced his awful relatives without a qualm, and that must have taken some doing. By all accounts, Devlin's father was even worse than his own ducal sire, and his father made Ivan the Terrible seem like a Sunday-school teacher. Nick had not been able to have a serious disagreement with her. She was not ambitious. There was no way of making Nick so unattractive she would turn away in disgust.

Or was there?

Everybody knew Nick had enjoyed an extended relationship with Bridget Fitzsimmons, a lesser light at Drury Lane. They had parted on the best of terms, and although they had not been lovers for more than a few years, Lord Nick still sent her flowers regularly for an important opening night. Bridie would be happy to do an old friend a favor.

Devlin returned to London late in the afternoon a mere ten days before the wedding. Pausing only to drop his luggage off at his rooms, he ran straight to his beloved.

Ladies Bradamant and Bellingham were in the midst of preparing for an evening party when he arrived, but Brad ran downstairs at once, her hair half up, half down, to greet him in the drawing room. His arms were open and ready. They spent a few minutes in breathless kisses before they could find words to speak.

They began in unison: "I have to talk to you."

"You first," Nick offered as they laughed.

"No, this is important. We need time, and Katy and I are off to a ball tonight."

"Must you?"

"I'm afraid so. It's one of Kate's bosom bows. They'd be terribly hurt if I didn't go. I believe I'm invited to settle a few scores with Mrs. Bagby," she explained.

"That old . . . witch. Oh, well, then I understand. But we must find time to talk. I have so much to tell you, Brad, that couldn't be said on paper. You'll be so proud of me. By the way, is this a new coiffure?"

"Oh, you . . . you . . ." she said good-naturedly, pretending to fume. "I have to run now. Nick?"

"Yes, love?"

"I'm glad you're back."

"I'm glad, too. Wait, love, is this the Castle girl's come-out?" She nodded. "I'm sure I have a card for that somewhere. I'll just run home, get into my evening togs and meet you there."

THE HONORABLE Mrs. Edward Castle, hostess of the evening's festivities, shared two major attributes with Lady Bradamant—her deep affection for Lady Bellingham and her enmity toward Drusilla Bagby. Thus it was that Mrs. Castle took particular joy in flaunting Brad's good fortune before her former employers. It was a richly rewarding experience. The Bagbys had treated Brad more like a slavey than a chaperon. Now that Brad was not only restored to her rightful position in society, but also engaged to marry the son of the Duke of Chance, they feared repayment for their years of cruelty.

Lady Bradamant was not so malicious, but she certainly meant to show them that the daughter of the seventh Earl of Hampton was not to be trifled with. The elegance of her lavender silk, appliquéd with a Grecian key design at the hem, and the sapphires at her neck and on her finger gave her confidence to face their sneering tongues. She smiled genuinely when they made pointed comments about Nick's absence, for she knew he was near.

"I must say, Bra-da-mant," the eldest Bagby daughter, now a plump and dissatisfied matron, enunciated carefully in a manner that made Brad wince, "I am surprised at you, when I think of how you used to describe Lord Nicholas to me, how you warned me never to have even the slightest conversation with him, how he was not to be trusted in the least. I can even remember all the tricks you said he would try—"

Brad interrupted her before she could continue. Truth to tell, she found reminders of Nick's rakish habits more disturbing than she liked to admit, but rather than show how the dart had struck home,

Lady Brad lifted her aristocratic nose in disdain. "My dear, I know now how much I wronged him. Lord Nicholas could always be depended upon to behave with the utmost courtesy and disinterest . . . with you."

Nick, entering the ballroom, could not hear the conversation, but he could tell that Bradamant had carried the field and the Bagbys were reduced to ignominious retreat. On his way to her side he accidentally brushed against a friend—Lord Ronald Graham.

"Nick, you're back! Just in time, too! This makes everything perfect."

Having caught Bradamant's eye, Lord Nick was not attending as he ought.

"Listen, Nick—oh, damn, I promised to push Northwood's spotty sister around the floor, and this is her dance. Listen, I won't have time to explain, but you'll know how to play along anyway, I expect. I don't know why we didn't think of this before, but it's not too late. Come by and celebrate later, all right?"

"Yes, yes, I'll see you later," murmured the inattentive lover, his eyes fixed on a dearer object.

Once he had reached Lady Brad's side, Nick remained glued to the spot. After the long separation, all he wanted was to be alone with Brad.

There was no chance to speak privately at the ball, or in the coach, where Lady Bellingham watched them carefully, on their return from the festivities.

Though he made light of it, Nick was actually exhausted, having traveled for four days over some of the worst roads in England. He was not prepared for an emotional scene.

"Will you come in for a while?" Brad asked him as their coach approached Lady Bellingham's house. She wanted desperately to talk to him, yet wished to take pity on his weariness. She could not help thinking, however, that it might be easier to gauge the truth with his reflexes somewhat slowed.

"Just for a minute," he agreed, hoping Lady Bellingham would relax her vigilance long enough for him to say good-night properly, that is, in a way the chaperon would consider most improper.

Unfortunately, there was an obstacle to pass before they could enter the house. Suddenly two small infants seemed to appear out of thin air and attached themselves to Lady Bradamant's lower limbs, piercing the air with loud, gusty sobs. A form once very familiar to Lord Nick stepped forward.

"Bridie!" he exclaimed in shocked surprise, and then wished he had not. Maybe there was no reason for this cold sense of pervading fear, maybe Bridie was just in such awful trouble that this was the only way she could seek help.

Miss Fitzsimmons, a soubrette, had always wanted to try meaty dramatic roles. This was her big opportunity. Tears trembled artistically at the end of her long lashes. Her long, dark tresses were unbound, as she had seen the famous Mrs. Siddons appear in

Lady Macbeth's sleepwalking scene. Keeping in mind that legendary performance, she held out her arms and cried out, in a faltering voice, "Oh, forgive me, my lady, but I didn't know what to do. It's not as if you don't know all about Nick, after all."

Nick was prevented from interrupting at this point by the infants, who released Lady Brad to attach themselves to him, crying out noisily, "Papa! Papa!"

"I always knew Nick would leave me someday. You must not think I want to take him away from you. I don't even ask anything for myself—but the children, my lady, my poor innocent babes! There was never much money, but now he says there is to be no more, none at all, and now with another on the way—" she actually managed a blush, touching her abdomen delicately "—now I'll have to leave my work for a few months and lose my own meager salary as well."

The actress's pleas were almost entirely drowned out by both Nick's shouted protest that it was all a lie, and a magnificent attack of the vapors enacted by Lady Bellingham. The ensuing noise prompted the butler to open the door so as to investigate the uproar, but unable to make sense of the tableau before him, he stood by and watched helplessly.

For a moment Lady Brad stood still as if in shock, coldly silent; then she recovered her poise. Over the din she somehow contrived to inform Nick that she had to calm Kate down and help her to her bed. She asked him to deal with Miss Fitzsimmons and her brood, then wait for her in the drawing room so that they could talk.

Devlin was seized with such fear as he had never before known. Here he had been thinking that his life was just beginning; surely it could not be all over now, shattered in a few devastating minutes.

IT WAS A STRANGER who greeted Lord Nicholas with deadly calm on her return. Lady Bradamant was in no state to listen to any explanations. Her hopes for the future, like Devlin's, had been raised by their warm response to each other in the past weeks. She had been lured into thinking so highly of him! She felt herself filled once again with the same anger that had possessed her when he had first proposed, only now it was compounded by the deepest hurt and disillusion.

Devlin, on the other hand, looked as if he had been through the mill. The children had started the damage by hanging on to his coattails, and he had completed it by loosening his collar, destroying his intricate waterfall by running his hands through his locks until his hair was almost standing on end.

"Brad, Brad, darling, it's not true. I swear it's not true." His voice was shaking. Distracted, he reached out for her hands, but they were limp in his grasp and cold as ice.

"Yes, I know," she replied, still standing stiffly.

"Thank God," he cried in relief, moving to take her in his arms.

She slipped away from him. "I've known it all from the very beginning. You need not have gone to so much trouble, Nick. I never meant to hold you to it."

This encounter had to be a nightmare. It could not possibly be real. He shook his head to clear his mind. "I don't understand. What do you mean, Brad?" he asked, half afraid of the answer.

"I am not a fool, Nick. I spent five years traipsing after those stupid Bagby girls, and I have heard every glib fiction there is. Even the one to get into a girl's good graces by proposing a marriage that is sure to be refused."

"Oh, no," Devlin groaned in genuine anguish.

"Oh, yes. Do you know, I really had not thought you would sink so low—to attempt to seduce a virtuous unmarried lady? So I decided it was time you learned a lesson you would not soon forget. I had planned to make you pay for your misdeeds— frighten you into thinking you would really have to marry me and then have you look like a fool when you were finally jilted. And you were frightened. I never saw such panic, or heard such excuses. Oh, yes, I recognized every single one. Well, you need not struggle anymore. Here is your ring. I will send the other presents back to you by messenger. I knew you really could not afford them. The announcement will be sent to the papers tomorrow. This is a new experience for you, isn't it, Nick?'' She met his unbelieving gaze. ''No woman turns down the great lover Devlin.''

Lord Nicholas felt as if he had been turned to stone. He wanted to scream, to cry, to shake her until her teeth rattled and then kiss her into submission, but he just stood there while she rang for the butler.

''Goodbye, Nick. Daniels will show you out.''

He wanted to get drunk, drunker than he had ever been, drunk enough to numb the pain. There was no one to turn to for comfort. Lord Ronald? Hadn't he suggested they get together tonight?

To celebrate, by God! Lord Ronald! *He* had engineered tonight's fiasco! It was his fault!

No. Bradamant's voice rang in his ears. This hell was of his own making. There was nobody to blame but himself.

Brad would never know how completely she had revenged herself. The word echoed in his brain over and over. Just for revenge. It was all just for revenge.

LORD NICHOLAS WENT on a right royal binge, maintaining a state of inebriation close to utter senselessness for a full week. That was no mean feat, as Devlin had a hard head when it came to alcohol. The return of his love tokens, however, slashed through the depths of his drunken stupor, and finally he broke down and wept, great heartrending sobs of despair.

Lady Brad had not forgotten a single thing. Floral bouquets he had sent her had long ago withered and faded away, but she returned all his other gifts: a delicately engraved posy-holder, an ivory fan, an embroidered workbasket, a Norwich silk shawl, a porcelain trinket box with an allegorical representation of Love after a painting by Angelica Kauffman, two gold serpentine chains and a diamond-and-sapphire hair ornament.

As he sobered up and his numbness passed, Devlin came at last to analyze that wretched parting and, indeed, their entire relationship. What had utterly broken his spirit was the thought that Bradamant had never cared for him at all, that she had been motivated solely by the desire to punish him. With his mental processes once more in action, he remembered one phrase—that she had not thought he would sink so low—and hoped against hope that this indicated some kind of respect. Even when they were engaged he had never really believed that she was in love with him, but he did think she liked him as a friend. That would have been enough to build a lasting relationship.

Her kindness at Chance, those few passionate encounters—those could not have been all lies. If he could only explain—but Lady Brad had removed herself from his reach. All his letters were returned unopened. The door knocker had been removed from Lady Bellingham's town house, and no one could or would tell him where the ladies had gone.

Devlin thought he had plumbed the depths of despair, but fate had not quite finished buffeting him. While Lord Nick was hoping in vain to track down his beloved and throw himself at her feet, bad news arrived once again from Yorkshire. Although Nick had just barely managed to rescue his estate from the ravages of a dishonest bailiff, he had no protection against either accident or nature. Fire, followed by severe gales and flooding, had virtually destroyed Devlin's small inheritance. The house was only slightly damaged, but the fir plantation was no more; the crops were blighted, the cattle decimated. Only by dint of hard work, and with the aid of capricious Fortune, could Devlin be saved from the poorhouse. He would have to return to salvage what he could, for in its present condition the land was not even salable.

Actually, hard work was most welcome at this time. Perhaps through sheer exhaustion he could find some measure of forgetfulness. But his anguish and loneliness were only intensified, for some weeks later Nick received the news that Charles, Marquis of Welting, had died in India of a nameless fever.

CHAPTER EIGHT

THE DISASTER Lady Bellingham had foreseen had come to pass, but it was not at all what she had anticipated. She and Bradamant had avoided the worst of the scandal and gossip by removing to the recently pacified Continent. While society buzzed with the news of Devlin's rejection—almost at the altar—Kate marched her companion through the churches and museums of three countries. But although Bradamant was known to be an indefatigable sightseer, it was obvious to the meanest intelligence that her heart was not in it. That most vital center of her feelings seemed to have stopped functioning the evening she said goodbye to Devlin.

Returning to London several months later, Brad discovered society still inclined to lionize the woman who had bested Lord Nicholas Devlin. More suitors than ever before sought her favor, intrigued by the challenge of succeeding where Devlin had failed. And Lady Bellingham made every effort to prevent the young woman from fading into the background. Sensing her companion's deep unhappiness, Kate tried her best to raise Brad's spirits by immersing her in all the functions of society at play.

In the midst of the social whirl, Bradamant finally lost the horrible mental inertia that had possessed her. Kate found no comfort, however, in observing Brad's frenzied pursuit of pleasure, since she perceived that these activities served only to mask an underlying sorrow. After that ill-fated night, the name of Lord Nicholas Devlin never once passed Brad's lips, not even to Lady Bellingham. To the public at large she gave no reason for giving Devlin his congé, which, naturally, led to great speculation among society gossips. Considering how many of Nick's adventures were openly known and had obviously been condoned by the mere fact of the young pair's engagement, the action that had terminated the relationship must have been correspondingly so much worse than anything that had been heretofore known about him.

Brad's worst fear was that Nick would come back to London. No one in town seemed to know where he was or where he had gone after that monumental drunk. The last anyone had seen of him, he had greeted a joking remark by his friend Lord Ronald Graham, in reference to his recovered freedom, with a swift uppercut to the jaw. He had left the boy unconscious on the floor of White's and simply disappeared.

If she ever had to face him again, Lady Bradamant did not know what she would do. She had discovered that revenge was not sweet at all. But she smiled and flirted with determination and energy. No one must ever know that the woman who had bested Nick Devlin had, after all, lost her heart to him.

IT DID NOT OCCUR to anyone that Devlin might be found on his own estate, since none of his friends had ever known him to visit the wilds of Yorkshire, and had he been seen at work there he would surely never have been recognized. Gone was society's darling black sheep, now a model landowner and diligent farmer.

The entire area was in a shambles after the fire and floods when he returned. Every penny that he had wrested from the dishonest bailiff—and it was a goodly amount—served to make only the most basic repairs. In order to finance further improvements, he was obliged to dispose of every available asset, even to stripping the manor house of furniture, silver, paintings and knicknacks.

Devlin even went so far as to sell most of his city clothes, no longer having any use for such formal evening attire as knee breeches and chapeau-bras. With the deepest sorrow he was forced to sell even the trinkets Bradamant had returned—but not her engagement ring. The rooms he had prepared for her arrival were likewise sacrosanct.

No amount of distraction, effort or sheer physical exhaustion could drive Bradamant from his mind. He did not really want to forget her, but it was hard, damnably hard, to be continually turning to someone who was not there. He had to prove to Brad that he was not as utterly worthless as she had thought. The hope that it might make some difference to her to know this could not be completely stifled.

For long months he worked like a dog, with no communication with the outside world, until finally a letter from his solicitors reached him.

The vicar was not at all surprised to see Devlin show up at the manse late on a storm-tossed evening. The two men had struck up an odd sort of friendship while working together to save the estate and the livelihood of some hundred people. Nick was prone to trudge the three miles to see the Reverend Mr. Fenster in all weather, especially when the ghosts in Bradamant's sitting room became too troublesome.

"Devlin, do come in. Your timing is perfect. I was about to demolish Sunday's sermon in a most un-Christian fit of anger. Here, let me take your wet things. Make yourself comfortable while I ring for some tea."

The vicar bustled about and spoke of trivial matters—parish gossip—until Devlin seemed ready to reveal his business.

"I've had a letter—well, really two—from my solicitors. It looks as if I'll have to go back to London, possibly for some weeks," Nick finally said.

"Is it good news or bad?"

"Oh, rather good, actually, except that I'll be stuck in town for some time. With luck, I may even be able to purchase that new equipment Dane was recommending.''

"A legacy?"

"Not exactly. Do you remember reading about that Indian nabob who was murdered in front of his own home?"

The vicar nodded. "Dreadful business."

"Yes, well, evidently he was a friend of my brother's, and Charlie had entrusted him with a wedding present for me." His voice was thick with suppressed emotions, for both Brad and Charlie. "You know how long it takes for news to travel. Charlie was dead before my message reached India that . . . that the wedding was off.

"Anyway, this old gentleman arrived in England with a package for me and was promptly set upon and killed. His household has been in an uproar ever since, I understand, trying to catch the murderers, so that it was quite some time before they found out for whom the package was meant. I don't know what it might be but, knowing Charlie, I suspect it must be valuable.''

"It is a pity that you should have to sell your brother's last gift to you."

"Yes, well, it can't be helped. And I don't need things to remember Charlie by. Apropos of which, I also have a letter from my sister-in-law. She and the children are coming back to England. They just waited so they could travel with another family with whom they are very close, but now everybody's ready and they should arrive about two months from now. Lady Welting has asked me to find a home for them in London and to keep an eye on things so that the duke cannot interfere in her arrangements.''

''I hear Chance is very ill, perhaps mortally so.''

Lord Nicholas ignored the vicar's comment and continued. ''I hope to be able to get this all done in short order, but just in case, there ought to be someone in charge to watch over the estate here. I don't want to make the same mistake I did with Harcourt.''

''I doubt that could happen again. If I may make the suggestion, Dane's eldest son would be an excellent choice. He knows the land, and he's had more book learning than most of the other country lads.''

''Yes, he's a good chap. I'll talk to him tomorrow; then I'll be on my way.''

''I hope all goes well for you in London. I will be praying for you.''

Even Lord Nicholas could not know how much those prayers would be needed.

CHAPTER NINE

ONE DARED NOT REFUSE an invitation from Sally Jersey. Not only did she wield considerable power as one of the patronesses of Almack's, that symbol of acceptance into the *haut ton*, but she was the most wicked gossip in all Europe. It would be just like Sally, Brad thought, accidentally to hit on the real reason for her absence and to spread it abroad. And perhaps word would reach whatever dark corner concealed Lord Nicholas Devlin. That possibility was to be avoided at all costs, so Bradamant grimly prepared herself for the ball as if she were going into battle.

True, nearly all of London held some particular memory of Nick for Brad, but Lady Jersey's home held a special significance. It was there, at one of her parties, that Nick had proposed marriage while plotting seduction. She could still recall exactly how he had looked, so humble yet passionate as he declared himself—and how dumbfounded when she accepted him!

No one could claim that Bradamant spared any effort in trying to exorcise the demon that haunted her. She allowed herself no time alone to brood.

There were dance partners aplenty and a minor court of admirers to surround her when she chose to sit one out. Only she could not help but compare their crude and clumsy attempts at dalliance with the soft words and amorous glances of one who was a past master of the art.

Bradamant was unhappy enough about the evening when, to add to her distress, during a moment when she was enjoying a short respite from the attentions of her suitors, Lady Bellingham suddenly chose to have a spasm.

"Trouble!" she proclaimed, like Cassandra of old. "I can feel trouble coming!"

In this case Lady Bellingham was perfectly correct, and one did not have to look very far for the cause. Lady Jersey, a mischievous gleam in her eye, was bearing down upon them with Sir Lucien Rendall in tow.

"My dear Lady Brad, this gentleman has been begging for an introduction to you. I could not believe you had never met before... with so many acquaintances in common. Let me present Sir Lucien Rendall to you. Sir Lucien, Lady Bradamant Mount-Aubin."

Lady Brad accepted his salutations politely and without interest. It was no mere coincidence that they had never met. Since returning to the social scene, Brad had assiduously avoided meeting the baronet, not so much because he was Nick's cousin, but because she could see for herself that Devlin's description of him as a "slimy, smiling snake" was no less than the truth.

"This moment was long delayed, Lady Bradamant, but well worth the wait," Sir Lucien said. "Yes, yes, I can see now how the invincible Devlin was conquered. For all his faults, which heaven knows are legion, Nick is extraordinarily perceptive."

Brad smiled with genuine amusement, thinking of Devlin's oft-spoken opinion of his cousin. The smile startled Rendall and Lady Jersey both.

Silence could keep silent no longer. "My dear, I am so glad to see that the mention of Devlin's name causes you no distress. Certainly after so many months you have the right to hope that that old scandal can be forgotten, but I fear with Devlin in town..."

If Lady Jersey hoped to be met with shocked dismay, she was doomed to disappointment. Lady Brad had herself well under control now. It was not even so bad, now that she knew. The real torment had been in waiting for the inevitable to happen.

"To tell the truth, I was surprised not to see Lord Nicholas before this. He has been out of town, I suppose," she said with a shrug.

"Where he has been I cannot discover," Rendall admitted, "but he is in London now. I've been searching for him for months, on behalf of his poor father."

Poor father? The Duke of Chance?

"It was only by the merest accident that I found him. Ran into him at Lincoln's Inn Fields while on an errand for the duke. I must say he behaved very oddly, even for Devlin—tried to avoid me at first!"

Lady Brad did not think that in the least odd.

"He was very closemouthed about his activities for the past months—and refused categorically to see his father, although that I have learned to expect.' Rendall shook his head sadly.

If he quotes, "How sharper than a serpent's tooth," I think I will scream, Brad thought.

He did, but she managed to restrain herself, albeit with the greatest difficulty.

"The duke is very ill, you know. If I did not have a number of commissions to execute for him, I would not have left his side at this time. The death of Lord Welting hit him very hard."

This time his words did provoke a reaction. Brad had been abroad when that piece of news must have reached London. "Charlie—I mean, Lord Welting—is dead? Oh, I am so sorry." Poor Nick. Looking back on their relationship, Brad hardly knew what had been deception and what had been real— except for his love for his brother. His death must have hurt Nick terribly.

"Yes, one of those tropical fevers. To think he seemed so hale and hearty, too, just a month before, when I left him."

Lady Jersey was becoming bored. She did not care for conversation in which she contributed less dialogue than anyone else. Only the hope of picking up some delicious tidbit of gossip could keep her quiet so long. Patience had its rewards, however.

Brad's next partner had come to claim her for the waltz when Rendall seized her hand and told her urgently in a low voice, "Devlin has returned for some purpose—one which he prefers to keep secret. This is no open return to society, to face down the gossips. And I ask myself what he has come back to do? You might ask yourself that as well."

Lady Jersey would do some asking, too.

It was not until four dances later that Lady Bradamant could steal a moment to pull her scattered wits together. She had put on a brave face before Sally Jersey and the insinuating Sir Lucien, but inside she was all turmoil. Air—that was what she needed, air.

The breeze was cool. It felt good against her feverish cheeks. At the end of the terrace she could discern, half-hidden in shadow, a couple stealing a kiss in the moonlight. Best not to think of Nick's kisses.

Would he try to see her, to talk to her? She could send his letters back as before, refuse him entrance to the house, but in the open, or in society? Any day, or night, he might step out of a crowd . . .

It was no use worrying about what would happen. Surely if she could maintain her composure before Silence Jersey, she could do it before Nick.

Time she was going back in. It was growing chilly, and her next partner would be looking for her. This was probably Lord Webly now.

A gentleman bowed to Lady Brad and held out his arm, his face hidden in the darkness. Thinking it was Lord Webly, she was just about to take the proffered arm when a sudden gust of wind caught the fringe of her shawl and tangled it in one of the flowering bushes that decorated the terrace. She turned suddenly to work it free, saving her life in the process.

The assailant struck down with such force that, finding empty air where he meant to strike flesh and bone, he fell forward to his knees. Lady Brad hardly realized what had happened until she saw the gaping hole that had been slit in the skirt of her most elaborately flounced French silk, a glamorous creation in periwinkle blue. As she opened her mouth in surprise, the man rose swiftly and brutally knocked her down, then disappeared into the night.

Her cry as she fell caught the attention of the courting couple. They helped the confused and shaken Brad to her feet. A blushing Miss Caldwell brushed off the dirt and examined the damage to the gown to see if it was slight enough to pass unnoticed. At that moment the stiletto, a wicked-looking blade, fell to the ground with a metallic ping. Miss Caldwell's screams brought everyone to the terrace.

Lady Jersey forced herself through the crowd. It was unthinkable for her not to be the first to know what had occurred, especially at her own party.

"What is it? What has happened?"

The sight of her mama and the patroness from Almack's quickly doused Miss Caldwell's hysteria. She tried her best to blend into the background.

But all eyes were on the disheveled Lady Bradamant. Some intelligent soul had brought a lighted candelabrum to illuminate the scene. Its clear flame revealed the weapon used in the assault. Brad could not tear her eyes from the hateful sight as she whispered in answer to Lady Jersey's question, "He tried to kill me."

SPECULATION WAS RIFE about the reason for the attack and the criminal's identity. Robbery could not have been the motive. Nothing had been taken—indeed, Lady Bradamant had been wearing no brilliants to attract the eye of a desperate man. What then? The lady's death would enrich no one. She was almost universally well-liked and had no enemies. The fear that London was faced with a murderous madman touched the *haut ton*, but before panic could spread, someone, somewhere, remembered that there was one person who had cause to wish Lady Bradamant Mount-Aubin ill, a person who was known to be violent, with more than a few duels to his discredit; a person, moreover, who had only recently been seen in London. People began to wonder anew what Lord Nicholas Devlin had done that was so unforgivable as to cause a well-behaved lady to jilt him mere days before their wedding.

The gossips' solution to the puzzle had not occurred to Lady Brad, nor did she hear at once the whispers that grew and spread about town. For some days she was in a state of shock, horrified and hurt to think that somewhere existed a man who hated her so much he wanted her dead. Her recollections of the attack were hazy in parts, but that sense of the attacker's enmity remained.

The Bow Street Runner came to question her, of course, as well as Lady Jersey. He was not pleased by her inability to describe the assailant.

"I'm sorry. I cannot say I even looked at him particularly, and it was very dark."

"Humph!" Lady Bellingham sniffed, sitting protectively close to her companion, as if she suspected the Runner of low designs. "Sally Jersey always keeps that terrace dark as pitch, so any lover who gets caught there cannot be recognized. I'm told that circumstance has saved any number of reputations."

"Did you notice anything at all about the man who attacked you, my lady?" The Runner, Albert Polk, persevered doggedly. He was a dapper little man with an air of being continually disappointed by life.

"Well, he was quite tall, I think...and he was dressed in evening clothes. I thought at first he was a guest."

The detective merely gave her a long look at this statement. "In which direction did the attacker run, did you see?"

"He went over the balustrade and into the gardens."

"Was any attempt made at pursuit?" He had a precise, almost pompous way of speaking.

"No, he knocked me down.... Only one couple saw him at all. By the time the others arrived on the terrace he had disappeared."

"Now, my lady, can you think of anyone who might have reason to wish you harm?"

"No!" It was a cry of great anguish. "I've thought and thought, and there just isn't anybody! I never hurt anybody; I never would. There just isn't any sense to killing me!"

The Runner paused a moment in thought, then decided to speak. "I have heard, my lady, that you were once engaged to be married, and that the wedding was called off very hurriedly. It is generally believed that your...former fiancé took his dismissal rather badly."

Brad stiffened, suddenly haughty. "*I* do not believe so. I have no doubt that, after careful consideration, Lord Nicholas realized it was all for the best."

Lady Brad's confidence was not shared by the Runner.

"Would you mind telling me, in strictest confidence, what was the cause of the estrangement between yourself and Lord Nicholas?"

"I am afraid I would mind, Officer, very much. But let me assure you at least that the estrangement was *not* due to any particular misbehavior on the part of Lord Nicholas. I am aware popular report has invented some scandal, of which only I supposedly know the details, to account for our separation. But it is not so. There is not, to my knowledge, any misdeed of Devlin's which was not common gossip long before ever we met."

The Runner was far from satisfied, but one could push a lady only just so far. Lady Bellingham, too, was showing distinct signs that the interview should be drawn to a close.

He rose to leave and politely, if insincerely, thanked the ladies for their help. At the door he made one last request. "By the way, Lady Bradamant, I would like to speak with Lord Nicholas just the same. His cousin saw him in town, I know, but we have not been able to find him yet. If he tries to contact you, you will let me know, won't you?"

His parting shot was most effective in disturbing the ladies' peace of mind.

BOW STREET HAD NOT yet found its way to the crowded middle-class boardinghouse in the suburbs where Devlin had elected to stay, but rumor had. Lord Nicholas had chosen the place, not only because it was cheap—a major consideration—but because it offered complete anonymity. No one there paid the slightest attention to the tall Mr. Nicholls, the name under which he had registered. He was obviously a gentleman, quiet and well-mannered. He knew that as long as he did not disturb the other tenants, they would not bother him. Nor was anyone from his former social set likely to discover his whereabouts, since he was no longer an object of interest, once he had descended to that neighborhood.

The inhabitants of that closed world of high society however, were of immense interest to the middle class, and the subject of great conjecture. They were as fascinating and seemed as remote as the native American Indian. Among Devlin's new neighbors Mrs. Yates was the chief informant circulating news of the upper classes, since she was related by marriage to a man whose best friend worked for Gunter's, caterers to the nobility.

One evening she was holding court before the front entrance to the boardinghouse, effectively blocking all traffic in and out, when Devlin returned, tired and harassed, from another session with the solicitors. Annoyed, but too polite to show it, Nick squeezed his way through the bevy of middle-aged gossips. Just as he reached the door, however, a familiar name struck his ears.

"Lady Bradamant Mount-Aubin. Funny sort of name that—Bradamant—don't you think? Sounds foreign. Not like a lady's name at all, neither. Well, it says here—'' she pointed a fat finger to an article in one of the more lurid scandal rags ''—a man tried to stab her, right in the middle of a big party. Given by Lady Jersey, it was.''

"Ooh, I've heard of her,'' another woman interjected. "Very powerful, she is.''

"And did they catch the killer?'' another asked avidly, hoping to hear reports of bloodshed.

"No, they ain't sure who it was. Or at least there ain't no proof.'' Her voice sank to a whisper, so that her audience could be in no doubt as to the impressiveness of her information. "Seems like the only person in the whole world with a grudge against this lady is an old beau she tossed out on his ear. A real rake, by all accounts, and one who don't take kindly to being laughed at, if you get my drift.''

Dear God, someone had tried to kill Brad! A mistake, it must be a mistake—but no, as Mrs. Yates had said, it was too unusual a name. The woman did say try, didn't she? Brad must be alive; she just had to be! But had she been hurt? He had to know. Even if he had to go back among society again, he had to find out.

It was only after some minutes of agonized thought that Devlin began to get the "drift'' of Mrs. Yates's final words. Did people really think he could hurt Brad? More important, did Brad think it?

DEVLIN'S NEXT VISIT to his solicitor showed how rampant suspicion of his guilt had spread. The lawyer seemed almost afraid to be alone with him and also made a point of mentioning that his firm did not handle criminal cases, such as murder.

One result of the lawyer's fear and desire to be rid of a troublesome client was that the matter of the late Lord Welting's gift was finally settled. With the utmost reluctance, the courts awarded one small package into Devlin's hands.

Charlie had been generous beyond expectation. Despite the close tie between the brothers, or perhaps because of it, Nick, ashamed to admit the truth, had never revealed the original circumstances of his betrothal. Instead, he had claimed true affection in his letter to his brother, unwittingly foreshadowing the depth of devotion he was to come to feel for Bradamant. Happily married himself, Lord Welting had been eager to do something special for his brother on such a joyous occasion. In a small leather sack he had sent a handful of bright stones—sapphires, diamonds, rubies, emeralds, amethysts and peridots—worth a small fortune.

Now these stones meant more than security for the estate. They also ensured Devlin of the funds to reenter society, not for amusement, but to see Bradamant at least once more, to prove his innocence—and to destroy the creature who had dared to assault her.

He was soon to discover that this would be no easy task. Seeking information, Devlin had gone to Bow Street and spoken with Brad's sad-faced Runner, Mr. Polk. During the conversation he not only learned that he was the preeminent suspect in terms of motive, but also realized that he had no alibi for the night in question.

As he began to return to previous haunts, the reactions of his former friends at first irked him, then enraged him. This was more than some silly bit of malicious gossip. People honestly believed he had tried to drive a stiletto into Lady Brad's heart. They avoided him in the street. Women who once longed for his attentions now ran from him in fear. To be condemned so completely, so ignorantly, made Devlin fairly tremble with anger. Fools that they were, by assuming that he had been the culprit, they were letting the real criminal go scot-free!

CHAPTER TEN

LADY BRADAMANT'S THOUGHTS were impossible to gauge. Despite Lady Bellingham's protective measures, Brad had heard the rumors, too, and they frightened her. She was quick to suspect that more than her own life was in danger now, and she was quite correct. Suspicion against Nick had reached such a fever pitch since the attempt on her life that his arrest was called for on all sides.

In self-defense Nick had felt obliged to change his address from his respectable boardinghouse to an inn, not at all respectable, in a far from salubrious part of the city. If he thought to avoid capture by such a ruse, he had greatly wronged the pompous Mr. Polk. That gentleman had assigned a less noticeable colleague to keep an eye on Lord Nicholas, and to pay particular attention to any attempt to change his base of operations or remove himself from the city.

Mr. Polk did not like this case at all. The aristocracy, of course, were always troublesome. Ten to one that even if you could prove a case against a nobleman, someone with power and money would see that he got off. Already someone was interfering in this case, probably the Duke of Chance, he thought. The magistrate had been ready to send out a warrant for Devlin's arrest when someone higher up had put the lid on it, temporarily.

Lack of proof bothered Mr. Polk. When he collared a man, he wanted the charge to stick. Neither did he relish the idea that he might possibly have made a mistake. Devlin was a puzzle. If he were to believe rumor, Lord Nicholas was the only man with a motive—revenge for having been jilted, made a fool of publicly and/or knowledge of a previous crime. If he were to believe Lady Bradamant's hints, Devlin was really relieved to be free of the entanglement. If he were to believe Devlin, the man was too crazy in love with the girl to hurt her. The nobleman was, however, capable of violence. No, no, Mr. Polk did not like this case at all.

The likelihood of another attempt was foremost in everyone's mind. There were signs that someone had tried to force entry into Lady Bellingham's house, but the new locks had proved too great a barrier. As had the second footman, who, hearing the noise, aroused the entire staff before going out himself to investigate, armed with a pair of dueling pistols belonging to the late earl.

Security measures were increased again after this scare. Two out-of-work pugilists were hired to patrol the grounds, and the locks were changed yet one more time.

Devlin had decided he must see Brad. It seemed to him, and it was not far from the truth, that everybody believed him guilty. Probably it was only a matter of time before they came and hauled him off to Newgate in chains. After that he would never see her again, unless she testified at his trial. The possibility that his ducal parent would exert himself on Nick's behalf never entered his mind. On the contrary, Nick's conviction and imprisonment would make it all the easier for Chance to try to take control of his grandsons' lives.

Which would it be—life imprisonment or transportation? Since Bradamant was still alive he might be spared the gallows.

They would know he was innocent if the villain succeeded after he had been put away. And a fat lot of comfort that would be!

The idea that Brad might believe him guilty was only a slightly less tormenting thought. She did not know how he had come to love her. Remembering how she had wreaked vengeance upon him, why should she think him incapable of returning the favor? Bradamant had to be told. He just had to make her see! How else would she think to protect herself against that villainous other?

That previous attempt against the Bellingham town house was not Devlin's work although he spent many nights observing the layout of the house and the routes and timetables of the guards. Nick meant to go directly to his target. He knew where Brad's bedchamber was. From the rear of the house he had seen at night that one room was the center of activity, carefully checked by guards before the lady retired. For a while Lady Bellingham had obviously spent the night on the daybed, keeping a light burning low, just in case she was needed, but was doing so no longer.

Brad's bedchamber was on the second floor—too high for any ladder. Her protectors had been smart enough to cut back the branches of a large oak near her small balcony, but had ignored the clinging vine some yards to the right. If the vines were strong enough to hold him for about twenty feet, Nick thought the building itself would afford enough purchase to complete the climb.

Twice the vines nearly pulled away from the wall, but somehow they managed to hold. Nick then used the ornamentation around a first-floor window to lever himself up. The climb took longer than he expected, and he was hanging from the balcony to the right of Brad's room when the guard came around on his second circuit. Suspended in space, Nick held his breath, but luckily the guard did not expect danger to come from above.

Once the man had moved on, Devlin hoisted himself up, breathing deeply in relief. He would not have been able to hold his breath much longer.

From the French windows of Brad's boudoir, Nick could see just the faintest gleam of light. In order to reach that window he would have to leap from one balcony to the other, a distance of some seven feet. It was an insane risk, but for his peace of mind he had to take it. His foot slipped as he leaped, causing him to fall short, only just able to grab the stone balustrade, grazing his hands until they bled, but saved from premature extinction. Beads of sweat broke out on his brow, but with one more pull he reached his destination.

He had fallen heavily, hoisting himself over the railing. Inside, Brad heard the sound with curiosity, but without alarm. Like the guards, she did not expect the villain to be capable of flight. She put down the book she had been trying to read and rose to investigate. She opened the windows and stepped out.

"Nick!" she cried out softly in surprised recognition, and cringed back a little. He was hidden in shadow, but she would know him anywhere.

"Please don't cry out!" he pleaded anxiously. "I won't move. I have to talk to you, Brad. Listen to me, please, that's all I ask. Just listen, I beg of you. I wouldn't hurt you, Brad, you have to believe that! Everybody's saying I tried to kill you, but it is not true! I could not! You must believe me!" Devlin was trembling with the force of his emotions. His voice was hoarse, almost unrecognizable, and he was close to tears. He had to make her understand, but she was just standing there, staring at him, terribly still and looking so frail he was frightened.

Her voice was low and calm. "I know it wasn't you, Nick. I never thought it was."

Having accomplished his purpose so easily and so quickly, Devlin was at a loss for words. He just stood there and drank in the sight of her. It had been so long since they were together.

Brad felt all her nerves on end as well. She, too, thought of the long months that had separated them, and how meaningless they had been.

"How are you feeling, Brad?" he asked hesitantly and conventionally. "Are you quite recovered? No one would tell me."

"Yes, I'm fine now. I wasn't hurt, just badly shaken."

"And I'm keeping you up. I'm sorry. I'd better let you get back to bed." But his feet were not willing to move.

Brad did not move, either, although she ought to have felt uncomfortable entertaining any gentleman, let alone Nick, in her night-rail. "I'm all right," she insisted.

"You are being careful, aren't you, Brad? I've been so afraid for you."

"Yes, I'm careful."

There was another long pause. Moonlight shone on them now, and Brad could see how the intervening months had left their mark on Devlin.

"You've hurt yourself," she cried, seeing the blood on his hands.

"Oh." He looked at them, unseeing. "I just scratched myself." He made little of his dangerous climb, quickly rubbing away the stains.

"You look so thin, Nick." Despite her careful control, Brad's voice was tinged with concern. "Have you been well?"

He opened his mouth to offer conventional assent, but the lies would not come out. "No, I can never be well without you."

It was impossible to tell who moved first. Suddenly they were in each other's arms, clinging with a kind of frantic desperation, as if they were afraid to let go and wake, finding it had all been a dream. They kissed, and it was the fireworks at Vauxhall all over again. Tears were streaming down Brad's face and were in Nick's eyes as well. Now that the dam had broken, the words began to flow, too, between kisses.

"Oh, Nick, I've been such a fool! Forgive me, please, forgive me!"

"No, you were right. I deserved everything. But I have learned my lesson. Only take me back and I'll show you. I love you so much. I think I loved you from the very beginning, only I was too stupid to see it."

"All the time I was so angry with you I never guessed why it was you had the power to disappoint me."

"Do you love me, Brad?"

"So much, so very much. I've only been half alive since I left you. Don't ever let me go again!"

"No, never," he promised.

Indeed, he was holding her as if he never meant to release her at all. They might have stayed out on the balcony indefinitely had not Nick suddenly bethought himself of the cold night air and the danger that might lurk there.

"You're shivering, Brad. You must be freezing."

"I never felt so well." The glow in her eyes seemed to indicate that her statement was true, but Devlin was more careful of her. He picked her up and carried her inside. Neither was ready to let go, however, so rather than setting her down on the chaise longue, Nick settled himself in a comfortable armchair, still holding his precious burden tightly in his arms. There was even a footstool handy for him.

"Better?" he asked.

Brad nodded her assent into the curve of his neck. "I'm all right, Nick. Truly. The knife didn't even touch me," she assured him. "It's just that I've had trouble sleeping."

And no wonder, after a vicious murder attempt, but with Brad in his arms again Nick had the strength of giants, and the confidence.

"Everything is going to be all right now, I promise you."

"Everything is all right—now that you are back."

"You're lumbered with me now." He remembered something, and squirmed a little to pull a certain token out of his pocket. It glowed and sparkled in the soft candlelight. "Brad?"

Without a word she held out her left hand for the ring. Nick slipped it on and kissed her palm.

He came to a belated recognition of the proprieties required of a gentleman.

"I ought to leave now," he said regretfully, making no effort to shift his burden.

"No!" Brad cried out. "Don't leave! Please stay with me, Nick." She tightened her hold.

"Here." He rested her head against his shoulder. "I'll tell you all about our home in Yorkshire. You relax and try to see if you can get some sleep."

The feel of his strong arms and the sound of his voice, deep and reassuring, were very soothing. Soon Brad's breathing, soft and regular, told Nick that she had nodded off. For a long time he watched over her, gently caressing her unbound hair, and then finally he, too, found rest in unaccustomed sleep.

SOME HOURS LATER, close to dawn, Albert Polk arrived at the Bellingham residence in a state of near panic. His associate had followed Nick to the vicinity of the house but, being far less clever than Nick, had been seen and chased off the grounds. When Devlin didn't reappear, the man went in search of his superior, who ran to the house, cursing fluently all the while, to demand audience with the countess immediately.

Lady Bellingham, with the Runner tiptoeing behind her, opened the door to Bradamant's bedchamber carefully and quietly. That room was empty, but seeing the door to the adjoining boudoir open, they moved silently to investigate.

Expecting a scene of blood and gore, Mr. Polk was nonplussed to find the supposed villain and victim entwined in a loving embrace, sleeping peacefully.

Lady Bellingham noted the contented smiles on their lips and the sapphire ring on the hand that still curled confidingly about Devlin's neck. Putting a forefinger to her lips, she hurried the Runner from this intimate tableau, pulling him out of the room and closing the door soundlessly behind them.

CHAPTER ELEVEN

IT WAS VERY NEARLY NOON before the lovers awoke, their long sleep a reaction to the emotional turmoil of so many months having at last been resolved. The question of who was trying to kill Bradamant retreated to the background of their thoughts in the light of their reunion.

Lady Bradamant woke first, experiencing a momentary confusion at finding herself so comfortably settled in a gentleman's embrace. But even half asleep, she knew beyond question that embrace to be Nick's. Remembrance of last night's revelations came flooding back, carried on a wave of pure joy. Nick loved her. Order had returned to the world.

In sleep he did not look at all like a wicked rake, but rather more like a little boy to be petted and protected. A perfectly fatuous smile was on his lips, inviting Brad's kiss.

Nick was not so unused to waking in the arms of a member of the opposite sex, but, like Brad, recognized his true love's touch at once. His eyes blazed passionately behind half-closed lids, the well-remembered Devil look, yet with a difference. With

Bradamant everything was different, more exciting, more real.

"Good morning," he greeted his beloved, and returned her kiss with interest.

"Good morning." She was too bemused to feel shy at their unaccustomed and unconventional intimacy. "This is nice. Will it be like this when we are married?"

He grinned wickedly. "Better. Much better. Just you wait and see."

They returned to their previous occupation with some enthusiasm until finally Nick found the strength of will to hold his love at a distance, or as much of a distance as can be accomplished when two people share a single armchair. "If we are to wait for the wedding, I think we will have to rise—at once!"

Brad rose, reluctantly but obediently. Watching Devlin pull himself out of the chair, she was filled with compunction.

"Oh, my poor dear! Are you terribly stiff? You should have awakened me."

He denied the stiffness vigorously. "I never felt better. But do you mean to say we might have removed to the bedchamber?" He certainly was feeling better if he was making indecent suggestions.

And Brad felt she must be quite as wicked as he, for the suggestion did not sound indecent in the least, but extremely attractive. She said as much.

"For shame!" He chuckled. "An adventuress, that's what you are—entertaining gentlemen in your room until . . . what time is it?"

She looked at the clock over the fireplace. "Good heavens, Nick, it's noon! I don't understand it. Someone ought to have come to wake me long since. Kate usually pops in half a dozen times a morning."

Nick's perceptive eye caught the one element out of place. He pointed to the closed door. "I think, my love, that we have already been found out. Now why, I wonder, didn't they rouse us?"

"I think Kate is being discreet. I'll have to go to her and explain, though she must have a very good idea of what is going on if she saw us together."

"Definitely! Madam, you have thoroughly compromised my honor," he accused her with mock stuffiness. "As a gentlewoman you are obliged to marry me to save my reputation!"

"Dear me! Well, I suppose I deserve no better for attempting to seduce a young gentleman of character," Brad joked, leaning forward brazenly in hopes of a kiss.

Devlin grabbed her shoulders but was, for the moment, more intent upon explanation than dalliance. "Brad, I wanted to explain about that first proposal, and about Bridie Fitzsimmons, too. You see . . ."

A finger to his lips, promptly kissed, stopped the flow of words. "You don't have to explain anything to me, Nick. I love you."

"But I want you to know. I was not quite as bad as you thought. I never really meant to seduce you...."

"Well!" Brad pretended offense.

"A...friend had made the statement that young ladies—the husband hunters—could not be seduced. Cynic that I was, I said yes they could, and offered to show how it is done. But I never meant to go through with it."

After sixteen years of watching the Duke of Chance at work, no wonder he had been a cynic, Brad thought. That would sour anybody. Another thought occurred to her. "But why me?"

Devlin smiled. "Because I was so sure you would not have me. You could have done much better for yourself. To my own knowledge there were at least two baronets and an earl, all well to pass, dangling after you."

"No, I could not have done better," she denied.

"Well, you could not find one who loves you better," Nick amended. "I finally realized it while we were at Chance. I was so happy with you. But then I was called away. Of course, Gra—this friend—knew my original proposal was a fake. He thought I still wanted my freedom. It was he who hired Bridie to give that little performance. I knew nothing about it, and was perfectly appalled when she started her scene! And ready to die when you turned me away."

"Oh, Nick." She was back in his arms again. "I was ready to die, too. I'd meant to give you a way out of it, but deep down inside I was hoping you would rather stay with me.''

''You never saw a man in such a hurry to be leg-shackled. What use is my freedom, or anything, without you?''

From this point the conversation reverted to such fond foolishness as would be tedious to relate, until they were interrupted by a timid scratching at the door.

''Who is it?'' Brad asked, without letting go.

''It's Kate, dear. May I come in?''

''Yes, love.'' She opened the door, prepared for a lecture.

''Oh, good, you are both awake. Nicholas, I have had your things put in the rose guest room, if you'd care to freshen up. Mr. Polk was so kind as to bring them over from your hotel,'' said Lady Bellingham, much aggrandizing the low establishment Devlin had honored with his custom. ''Just ring and the foot-man will bring you some hot water. There's nun-cheon in the dining room as soon as you are ready.''

Thus dismissed, Devlin obeyed orders in a state of great puzzlement, but encouraged by a comforting handclasp from Lady Brad.

Left alone with Lady Bellingham, Brad rushed to her with a swift, enveloping hug. ''Oh, Katy,'' she said, holding her friend tightly, ''I am so hap-py!''

NUNCHEON TURNED INTO a celebration. The butler, blessed with that sixth sense the best servants always possess, brought out the vintage champagne.

As the lovers seemed too bemused to make plans, Lady Bellingham felt obliged to give a little hint. After all, they had spent the night together, however innocently. Not that she had any doubt as to their intentions, but weddings did not happen by accident.

"Well, my dears, and have you picked a date yet?"

The lovers looked at each other and burst out laughing. Lady Bellingham looked confused for a moment and then she, too, joined in the merriment. She had made them name a date the last time as well. It was nice to know they could all laugh about it now, after so much unhappiness.

"I don't suppose it still counts that we've had the banns read twice already?" Nick asked. "Oh, well, I don't want to wait even one more week! We can be married tomorrow, by special license. Lady Bellingham, are you by any chance acquainted with any bishops?"

"Several. Actually, my cousin Percy is secretary to the Archbishop of Canterbury. I will write you a letter of introduction."

"Yes, I suppose I'll need one. I would not want to be turned away from the doors. Well, what say you, Brad?" He turned to her with a confident smile. "Will you marry me tomorrow?"

Lady Brad was suddenly serious. She paused a moment and said firmly, "No."

Her auditors exclaimed in distress, "No? Brad, what do you mean?"

"I don't understand."

"No, I will not marry you in some hole-and-corner fashion. Don't you understand, Nick? My jilting you before had all society gossiping about us—and laughing at you. I won't have that. I want everybody to see how much I love you."

"Oh, darling," he cried, moved by her generosity, "that doesn't matter. All that matters is that we take the vows that will make you mine. I've waited so long. I don't think I can bear to wait much longer." Nick could not very well say before Lady Bellingham that the passion that burst forth at their every embrace could barely be held in check, but Bradamant understood very well without any words.

"Nor I, Nick. But I want to do more than just make up to you for the embarrassment I caused you. The gossips are not laughing now. They are saying you . . . well, you know what they're saying. I won't let them. I want everybody in London to see me make those vows to you. I want them to see that I believe in you, as well as love you. I want them to see that there is no reason in the world for you to . . . hurt me."

Devlin was deeply touched. After a slight pause Lady Bellingham agreed. "She is quite right, Nicholas."

"I suppose so," he concurred reluctantly, "but how long...?"

"Only ten days, Nick. We can make all the arrangements in that time, can't we, Kate?" She pleaded for consent.

Lady Bellingham gulped, shuddered and then nodded.

"It won't be much notice, but everyone will come, if only out of curiosity. I will even invite that old sourpuss Mrs. Bagby. Yes, and my cousin Hampton, too!"

CHAPTER TWELVE

LADY BRADAMANT and Lord Nicholas made quite a few public appearances in the week preceding the wedding. They attended two evening parties, and were seen together daily in Hyde Park, as well as visiting the British Museum to see the Elgin marbles, watching a balloon ascension and viewing the latest exhibit at the Royal Academy.

These appearances were reaping beneficial results. It was quite easy to suspect Devlin of every imaginable crime when one had not spoken to him for months on end, and then only to have seen him from a distance, looking fierce and brooding. Once reacquainted, one remembered what fun Devlin was—both his wicked sense of humor and the way he had of making one feel quite extraordinary. If tales of previous violence were recalled, there were now those who remembered such important details as why it had happened—like the time he had beaten Gervaise Edwards to a pulp, for striking a defenseless woman. People also remarked that Lady Bradamant was nobody's fool to be taken in by a recognized rake and seducer. To say that all suspicion against Devlin had been lulled would be utterly false, but a nagging doubt now existed in most minds. It would no longer be taken as fact that Nick was the would-be murderer.

Whatever they believed or suspected, everyone who had received one of the much-desired invitations decided to attend. No one wanted to miss the wedding of the season. Rumor whispered that even the Prince Regent meant to attend, the very thought of which sent Lady Bellingham into a tizzy.

Saturday morning dawned bright and clear, the sun obviously willing to do its part in making the day perfect for the lovers. Brad's wedding dress was simple in design, a lovely white peau de soie, shot through with gold threads, seed pearls ornamenting the bodice. Her beauty today, though, owed more to an inner glow of happiness than to her attire and flattering coiffure.

Nick had been sent to St. George's early, where he was quickly driving his best man—Lord Ronald Graham—into a nervous breakdown. If gentlemen could have the vapors, Graham would have done so, and he privately swore to himself that he himself would never go through such an ordeal.

After what seemed like hours of waiting, Devlin and his best man were finally signaled to come to the front of the church, and to the music of George Frederick Handel, Lady Bradamant came down the aisle to take her lover's arm. Neither of them noticed the church, filled to its rafters with guests, or the beautiful way Lady Bellingham had decorated the altar with flowers. Quietly and firmly they made their vows. Only after they had left the church, now husband and wife, did they reawaken to the existence of others, recalled to earth by the sobs of Lady Bellingham.

"I'm so happy for you," she cried gustily, hugging them both.

"Now, now, Katy." Devlin comforted her with gentle pats on her back, just as one might croon to an infant. "You know the old saw. You're not losing Brad, you're gaining me. Why, I only took Brad because you were part of the bargain. I never had a mama, you know."

"You see how it is, Brad. I warned you. The man simply has to have lots of women around to flirt with, regardless of age," Lady Bellingham joked, laughter mingled with her tears. In the past she had had mixed feelings about Devlin (of which he was well aware), further confused by palpitations, but now he had become a dear friend. She could have loved him for the happiness he brought Bradamant alone, but she was coming to love him for himself as well.

Lady Bellingham's oversized grand ballroom was for once the right size to accommodate the hundreds of guests who arrived for the wedding breakfast. She had accomplished miracles in ten days. Admittedly the room itself, modeled after the famous Salle des Glaces in Versailles, was magnificent. Bouquets with long streaming ribbons gave the room color and warmth. A new firm of caterers had been hired and, in order to make their reputation, had outdone themselves. The late Lord Bellingham's cellar was divested of its choicest wines, sending more than one oenophile into ecstasy, since the earl had been a famous connoisseur.

The boudoir into which Nick had stolen ten nights before had been transformed temporarily into a dressing room for him. After dispensing with the services of the aged butler, who had demanded as his prerogative the opportunity to be valet to the bridegroom, Nick knocked on the connecting door, strangely nervous. A soft voice bade him enter.

Brad, too, had sent away her maidservant. She was seated at her dressing table, wearing a silken negligee with lace trim, her soft hair falling loose about her shoulders. Her eyes were innocent and trusting.

After gazing at her hungrily for an interminable moment, Nick took his courage in his hands and advanced to where she rose to meet him. He put his hands on her shoulders gently, almost shyly, and confessed in a voice fraught with emotion, "Brad, I'm nervous—scared."

She smiled at him with eyes full of love and faith. "I'm not. I love you, Nick."

"I love you, Brad."

And then he swept her into his arms, and soon forgot to be nervous.

CHAPTER THIRTEEN

IN THE DARK HOURS of the night, when even the lovers had succumbed to sleep, wrapped in each other's arms, a sound, as of breaking glass, pierced the nocturnal silence.

One of the legacies remaining to Devlin from his years with the Royal Navy was the ability to wake swiftly at any noise, immediately alert. For a moment he was distracted by the sight of his wife, sleeping peacefully, pillowed against his shoulder, but another sharp creak brought him to abrupt attention. Listening carefully he heard cautious steps in the adjoining boudoir-cum-dressing room. Obviously, someone had copied Nick's method of illegal entry.

In a second, Nick roused his sleeping wife and, with his hand over her mouth to keep her silent, bundled her under the bed. After swift rearrangement of the bedclothes, he followed her.

Brad had not long to wait to learn the reason for this strange behavior. Nick had barely dived under the bed when they heard the door to their chamber open very softly and slowly. This was followed by the barest whisper of footfalls, the slight clatter of the bed-curtain rings as they were pulled aside, and then the horrifying sound of a sharp blade slashing through material.

Evidently the would-be murderer sensed something odd, because he stepped back with a throttled cry of surprise and outrage. Before he could take another step Nick was upon him. The two men thrashed about the room, knocking over chairs, grunting and straining against each other. From beneath the bed Brad heard several blows strike home with sickening thuds but had no idea whom they struck. She dared not rise from her protected position for fear of getting in Nick's way or distracting him. The clatter of the knife as it dropped announced that at least one danger was eliminated.

Now the attacker was intent not only upon escape, but was also trying to dodge Devlin's punches. He was no match with his bare fists for Nick, who had trained under Gentleman Jackson. The darkness, which prevented Devlin from seeing both his opponent and the terrain, had been his only ally. Even then Nick had been able to take hold of his left arm and twist it back in a frightful grip until the pressure became unbearable for his assailant.

They had nearly reached the open windows when the gentle moonlight cast its glow over the struggling pair. This was the moment Nick had been waiting for, hoping to see the villain's face finally and identify him. Instead, all he saw was a face out of a nightmare, grotesque and unbelievable.

A moment later Nick realized the attacker was wearing a mask, but that split second was all the evildoer needed. In a flash the masked man had slipped from his grasp. Making a desperate lunge for freedom he grabbed a small night table with his good arm and threw it in Nick's path.

By accident, the villain had chosen better than he knew. Atop the table had been a pretty jar of colored marbles, which broke and spilled its contents over the floor. Suddenly Nick was flat on his back, knocking a chair over on top of himself. From that uncomfortable position he saw the villain run out the windows and over the balustrade, grabbing a rope and twisting it around his right arm. He was gone, and Devlin had not even seen in which direction he had fled.

The sound of fluent cursing in a familiar voice finally lured a worried Bradamant out from under the bed. She ran into the other room, nearly meeting disaster herself on one of the spilled marbles. Gratefully she noticed that her new spouse was not so much injured as blazing angry.

"Damn! I had him right in my hands!" he wailed, holding out his palms, empty. "And I didn't even get a look at his face! He was wearing some bloody ghastly mask!"

"Are you all right, Nick?" Brad asked, seized once again by fear. There was blood on his face from a cut on his cheek, and a great deal on his hands. She found a kerchief, wet it and rushed forward, avoiding the marbles, to attend to his wounds.

"I'm fine, love. I'm not hurt," he assured her. "And you're all right, too. That's the important thing. But, oh, to come so close, and fail through sheer clumsiness!" Watching Brad tending his hands with gentle care, he told her, "Not to worry, sweetheart. That's not my blood, but his. I think I broke his arm," he announced with no little satisfaction. "He won't feel up to trying that again for a little while."

The sounds of the struggle had evidently penetrated the lower reaches of the house, as footsteps could be heard pounding up the stairs. Brad helped Nick into his dressing gown and then answered the door. Lady Bellingham, her face covered with cucumber lotion and wearing one of the late earl's most extravagant dressing gowns, led a troupe armed with such varied weapons as a skillet, an antique musket, a broom and a hatpin.

"Brad, Brad, are you all right?" she cried.

"Yes, we're both fine. Oh, Kate, you should have seen how clever Nick was. He saved us and he pummeled the villain, too, only the man escaped."

"You see how clever I was—to let the bas—attacker—get away." Nick was still angry with himself.

Lady Bellingham had her priorities in better order. "You and Brad are alive and unharmed. I do not call that stupid."

"Daniels," Nick addressed the butler, "will you find out what happened to the guards—if they are unhurt, or if they have seen anything? If they are all right, I want one of them stationed under this balcony." He sent one of the footmen to fetch the rope still dangling from the balcony, warning him against the marbles.

"Oh, dear, that was George's collection. I always thought they looked so pretty." Kate picked up those she could see. The housekeeper began to use her weapon to sweep up the shards of broken glass.

Devlin requested that all the doors and windows be checked, and all the rooms as well, to make sure that the man had not sneaked back in. When the house was pronounced secure again, they returned to their respective beds once more. Nearly all found sleep strangely elusive.

Nick, lying there deep in thought, running his fingers absentmindedly through Brad's curls, came slowly to realize that his wife, too, was wide awake, pensive. *This is not the proper behavior for a wedding night,* he thought.

He proceeded to behave properly.

CHAPTER FOURTEEN

LATE IN THE AFTERNOON Lord and Lady Nicholas
Devlin were interrogated by Mr. Polk about the preceding night's disturbances.

"I suppose I must have heard the glass breaking," Devlin explained. "Anyway, suddenly I was
wide awake. There was a creaking noise and footsteps, moving very slowly. I didn't stop to think. I
just grabbed Lady Nicholas—" this with a private
smile to his bride "—tucked the sheets around the
bolster and dived under the bed. Just in time, too."

Bradamant, who was holding his hand, shivered
at the memory.

"He stabbed at the bedclothes, and I jumped him
from behind. But he managed to trip me up and get
away. When I got a look at that awful mask he was
wearing, I must have loosened my grip on him."
Nick still felt very badly about letting go of the
criminal.

Mr. Polk grabbed hold of one salient detail. "You
say he wore a mask?"

"Yes, a terrible and weird thing, like a hallucina-
tion conjured up by an opium eater's disordered
faculties. Unreal, and not quite human."

"You would recognize it if you saw it again?"

"Most certainly."

The Runner made notes in his occurrence book and smiled. He had a little idea about that mask. His eyes met the hopeful gaze of the victims. That guess must remain secret for a while longer, but the sight of adhesive plaster on Devlin's forehead produced another thought.

"Hmm," he said provocatively, "that must have been quite a struggle?"

"Yes," Nick answered laconically, not wishing to dwell on what he considered a complete failure.

"It was awful," Bradamant elaborated. "I could hear the blows strike home, and when I went to join Nick he had blood all over his fists."

Mr. Polk looked at the fit, athletic figure of Lord Nicholas and was glad that he had not been at the receiving end of the famous Devlin right. "May I take it as understood, then, that the assailant also wears some souvenir as a result of the encounter?"

"You may. In fact, I doubt he'll be able to show himself in public for some little time. I'm sure I broke his arm and at one point I think he may have fallen on his knife. That's where the blood came from."

"This will bear investigation. A broken arm, as well as various cuts and bruises, cannot be hidden. We shall see if any of the gentry claim to have been attacked by footpads last night."

After the Runner had made his correct adieux and bowed himself out the door, Nick observed, "Our little friend has something up his sleeve. He'll turn something up, you'll see."

"Oh, I hope so." Brad turned into the comfort of his embrace, burying her face in his shoulder. "It's not just that I'm so afraid—for you, too, which is worse—it's knowing that there is someone who hates me and wants me dead.... Why?" she cried out. "What have I ever done that someone should want to kill me?"

Lady Bellingham, entering the room, caught sight of their cozy position and tried to make a discreet and silent exit, but was called back by Devlin.

"Don't leave, Kate. We need you. It is about time that the three of us put our heads together and puzzled this thing out."

She rang for tea, her usual aid for the analysis of problems, and took an adjoining chair. "Oh, I have thought and thought, Nicholas, but I just cannot think of anyone who could have *that* kind of grudge against Bradamant."

Devlin considered this for a moment, then came upon an idea. "But why does it have to be a grudge, as you call it? We have all had our minds on that kind of motive because of the suspicions against me, but it has never really been very likely. After all, Brad, who would you say are the people who like you least?"

"The Bagbys," she answered without hesitation, "and my dear cousin Hampton. They know they treated me badly and rather than feel guilty they blame me. And, of course, they are petrified I'll talk about them. You will have noticed that the earl has been conspicuously absent from town since I've been here."

"You see what I mean—the average petty jealousies of society. It might easily lead to malicious gossip, perhaps even to a rather nasty practical joke, but not murder."

"That is true," Brad agreed, a little relieved. "But what reason could there be? What would anyone gain?"

"Well, let us try to look at this logically. What would be the result? What would be different if you died?"

Lady Bellingham said the first thing that came into her head. "I should have to hire a companion."

"You would have had to do that anyway—will have to—once Nick and I go off to Yorkshire."

"And I would have to change my will."

"That's so sweet of you to leave me something, Kate, but it would hardly be enough to... Kate! You didn't!"

The gentle widow defended herself vigorously. "Well, why shouldn't I? It is my money! And I have the right to leave it to whomever I wish. Besides, there is nobody else."

Nick leaned over and dropped a kiss on her forehead. "Hush, both of you. The money is not important to us. But it could be to someone else. Kate, who is the residuary legatee?"

"The what?"

"Who gets the rest? Or the whole thing if Brad does not?"

"Oh, a home for unwed mothers."

"Rats! Well, I refuse to suspect unwed mothers. What about your money, Brad? Who gets that?"

"You do, now. Before that it was the unwed mothers again, I'm afraid. Not that my little competence makes much of a motive."

"Any amount of money can be motive, if you're desperate enough. What else?"

"Perhaps Brad knows something that could destroy someone's reputation, or send them to jail," Lady Bellingham suggested excitedly. "Remember the way people were sure she knew something absolutely dreadful about you, Nick? Something like that."

Brad did not think much of that idea. "You've been reading Mrs. Radcliffe again," she accused her. "That sounds like the plot of a gothic novel."

"But it's not a bad idea." Nick defended the widow. "Although I don't think it is likely. I had another idea. It ill becomes me to mention your other suitors, but I know I was not your only offer. Did any of them take their rejection in bad part?"

"No. I won't mention names, because it ill becomes me to boast, but there were no hard feelings. It was generally assumed that my experience with you had left me overly cautious. A few continued to court me, and two are now affianced to other ladies."

"Pity. I had hopes for that idea. I don't like to complain, but I think we must face the fact that the murderer seems to have no objection to dispatching me as well. A rejected lover might be madly jealous of my success."

" 'If I can't have you, nobody can,' " she quoted melodramatically. "Really, Nick, I think you've been reading gothics, too."

Intently serious of a sudden, Nick said in a low voice, "If you had died I doubt I would have survived much longer."

Brad was moved, but determined not to be sentimental. "If I had died you would certainly not have survived. Because you would have been hanged from the gallows." All at once the implications of what she had said sunk in. "Nick, that's it. I'm not the real victim at all. It is you the murderer wants dead."

"But...but that makes no sense." Nick resisted the idea strenuously. "It's far too complicated. And hardly a sure thing. I might not have been convicted of the murder."

"Do you really think so? Personally, I think you would have been lucky to survive the trial without being lynched out of hand, considering the tone of the gossip I overheard. And I was probably protected from the worst of it!''

Devlin turned to Lady Bellingham to refute the charge but was disappointed by her reply. ''I always thought there was someone behind those rumors, someone fueling all the animosity and fear toward you, Nicholas. I took it for a cover-up measure on the part of the attacker, to keep suspicion away from himself. But perhaps Bradamant is right and there is more to it than that.''

''Nick, just consider. If you were going to commit a murder, how would you go about it?''

''Make it look like an accident—runaway horses, a fall downstairs. He might fall, strike his head and drown when fishing....'' Devlin gave a few ideas, just as they came to him.

Lady Bellingham stopped him before he could continue. ''Please, no more! Really, you know, Brad, everyone should have realized that Nicholas was innocent. He never would have been so clumsy as to fail.''

The recipient of this dubious praise burst out laughing. ''And two times, too! When I come to think of it, our murderer has been remarkably ineffectual!''

''Let us hope he continues so!'' Brad chided him for unseemly levity, while trying to conceal a smile. ''But if his execution is faulty, his planning seems extraordinarily clever to me. Nick, don't you see? If he had just wanted to kill me, he could easily have engineered an accident of some kind, and no one would have suspected a thing. Instead, he takes very great care that the 'murder' is recognized as such—takes incredible chances, too. It cannot have been to no purpose!''

Nick was forced to agree. ''You know, when I first heard of the attack on you, all I could think was that it was a mistake. No one could want to kill you. It appears I was right.''

''You won't deny that there are a few people who would not grieve at your passing?''

''A few? My enemies are legion!''

''Don't boast, Nicholas,'' Lady Bellingham tut-tutted.

''No. I'm not proud of it. Some of them no doubt have reason to hate me.''

''That's the one thing I don't understand, Nick,'' Brad interrupted. ''I could feel the hate behind that attack. He...he truly enjoyed trying to drive that stiletto into me. Do you think he's insane?''

''No. That hatred you felt could have been meant for me as well. If he had had even the slightest idea what you mean to me...of course, he would have enjoyed hurting me like that. To send me to the gallows afterward would have been nothing in comparison.''

''But how could anyone know how you felt, when even I did not?''

"Chance knew. I think he realized it before I did. And Lady Rendall would have seen it, too. What she knows, my cousin Lucien knows."

"And Sir Lucien Rendall loves to gossip."

"Exactly. You're right. The villain could not have thought of a better plan to put me through hell. But what now? Obviously he can no longer count on my being convicted of your murder."

"No, he has to kill us both now," Brad suddenly realized.

As she was becoming increasingly upset, Devlin spoke words of comfort. "He will not find it very easy. In fact, the longer it takes, the more trouble our murderer is going to have. People have had time to think, so any motive that is proposed will be much more carefully scrutinized. Also, two failures are bound to have caused some irritation of the nerves, which means that he will be far likelier to make mistakes."

"I hope so. And now I have you to protect me. He has discovered your strength to his cost."

Devlin was not about to reveal his present fear. Brad was quite correct in supposing him capable of overpowering their assailant in hand-to-hand combat, even if the villain had the use of both his arms. However, a pistol need not be used in close quarters to be fatal. And poisoned chocolates could be delivered by post.

"Yes," he agreed, "and now it is too late to engineer an accident, as he might have done in the beginning."

"What do you think he will do now?" Lady Bellingham asked.

"Wait," Nick answered with assurance. "It may be our biggest advantage. He's injured, remember. I doubt very much Mr. Polk will discover a broken arm in London. But a list of gentlemen who have retired to nearby estates might prove interesting reading. He'll be recouping his strength, and he will have to rethink all his plans now, too."

"But, Nick, there isn't much time for him to wait. As soon as your sister-in-law is settled, we will be going home." Home—what a lovely word. Brad had not known a home of her own since she was sixteen.

"And Ann and the children should arrive in a matter of weeks."

"Why are you so sure it must be done in London?" Lady Bellingham wondered.

"The one thing Brad was sure of was that the attacker was a gentleman. Obviously, here in London he is so much a part of the social scene he is virtually invisible. However, in the wilds of Yorkshire any stranger would be immediately suspect."

"So, what then?"

"I still believe he will need a little time to plan. Remember, his whole strategy has to be changed. But as soon as he has done that, he will be back to the fight."

"We must be prepared for him when he does," Brad said decisively, secure in her faith in her husband.

"But how?"

"You said someone was manipulating gossip before, Katy," Devlin replied. "Well, so can we. With a word in the right ear, all society can become guardians of our safety. You can be a big help there, Kate, because people believe you implicitly."

"I know how to do it, too. Just you leave it to me."

"Now that we are looking in the right direction, we should be able to deduce who is the source of our danger—with the special help of Mr. Polk," Brad added.

"And then we can set a trap for our would-be murderer," Nick declared with a determined gleam in his eye.

"Before he sets one for us," said his down-to-earth bride.

CHAPTER FIFTEEN

THE FIRST PART of their plan was easy to put into practice. Nick felt that he and Brad would be safest in a crowd. And in any crowd in fashionable society, Lady Jersey was sure to be seen.

"But my dears, on your wedding night! This man is a villain!" Murder was merely titillating, but to interrupt one's amours was a cruelty she could recognize and appreciate. "And you say he meant to kill you both?"

"He could hardly kill one without the other."

"No, I suppose not." She leered knowingly. "Do you think it might have been a jealous suitor of Lady Nicholas's?"

"You flatter me, Sally," Bradamant told her. "Honestly, can you imagine me femme fatale enough to inspire that kind of passion?"

"You were woman enough to win Nick Devlin," Sally said knowingly. Mentally she reviewed Brad's former suitors. No none of them were capable of that kind of passion. "Have you no idea what the reason behind these attacks might be?"

"None," Brad answered mendaciously.

"All we can be sure of is that he'll try again."

Lady Jersey shivered.

The Devlins let Lady Jersey mull over this information a little while, waiting for it to return to them in whispers. Then Lady Bellingham entered the fray to do her part.

It was three evenings later, at a rather dull party given to celebrate art collector Cavendish-Smythe's latest acquisition, that she was given her chance. Examining what was left of a Roman sculpture of Neptune, she merely waited for Lady Jersey to approach her. Following preliminary conversation about the poor quality of the entertainment, edibles and even decoration, Lady Bellingham allowed Lady Jersey to lead into another topic closer to home. In the middle of their comfortable cose, the amiable widow imperceptibly took control.

"Sally, who would want to kill Nick?"

"Nick? But it's...oh. Devlin *does* have a few enemies. Let me see. Well, Gervaise Edwards—he's never forgiven Nick for that beating he took. Devane—he lost his wife and a duel to Nick. I know, it was an Italian fencing master she ran off with, but it was Devlin who opened his eyes to the truth about her. There are others. But not everyone who hates him would necessarily turn to murder. I doubt anyone hates him more than his own father, but even the Duke of Chance would not murder his son. Besides, I hear the old man is too feeble, about to breathe his last," she added as an afterthought.

By this means Nick and Bradamant had the *haut ton* in its entirety puzzling over their attacker's identity. Through Sally Jersey they had successfully turned suspicion from Devlin to Devlin's enemies.

The sense of time ticking away was oppressive to the newlyweds. They knew another attempt must soon be made, and each was desperately afraid for the other's safety. Devlin tried to hide his concern by distracting his wife's attention from their endangered situation by a flurry of activity in preparation for his sister-in-law's arrival.

Viewing the fifteenth town house in four days, Bradamant was very nearly too exhausted to worry about possible murder attempts. Once more she forced her tired limbs upstairs and down, but no matter how many times she counted, there were simply not enough rooms.

"No. It is not large enough," she wailed. "They are none of them large enough!"

"Two of the children will be at school. Soon a third," Nick reminded her.

"They still need a place to come home to. You know, the next time you are pumping Sally Jersey for information, you ought to find out if she knows of a place. She hasn't discovered anything else of any help," Brad commented.

Nick came up behind her and massaged her weary shoulder muscles. "You are not to worry about that, do you hear? You have a husband to take care of you now, and the cunning Mr. Polk is on the job. Besides, there is not time. If we don't get to work, Lady Welting and her six little Devlins will be setting up house in Hyde Park.''

''If I could think of a single house in London that was the right size, I think I would scare the present tenants into selling,'' Brad said mischievously.

''Well, come on. The next one the agent told us about sounds a little more hopeful. Let's give it a try.''

In the carriage, traveling to see the next house on view, Devlin commented, ''It's a pity things aren't different. Ann really should have the use of Chance House, which is more than large enough, but that would only give the duke greater opportunities for interference. To tell the truth, I'm more than a little surprised that he has not tried anything yet. It's not like him to let his heir escape his clutches. But I've had my solicitor on the lookout for any funny business, and he says nothing has even been hinted at.''

''Perhaps the rumors are true, and he really is too ill to fight. Your cousin Lucien as much as said he was dying. . . .'' She shrugged.

''From the way he ran back home it could be true. Lucien would never miss being at the duke's deathbed,'' Devlin said sarcastically.

''If that's the case, though, Chance will belong to young Charles very shortly. Instead of buying, shouldn't we rather rent a place for them?'' Brad suggested.

"Ann did specifically ask for a house to be purchased in her name."

"I wish I had a better idea what she wants, other than a place big enough to hold her brood."

"I'll show you the letter when we get home," Nick offered.

This next house was, thank heaven, large enough, although it had not been kept up as it ought. It would need quite a bit of work. Although Brad wanted to read Lady Welting's instructions for herself before they completed any sale, the fact that they had at least found a sufficiently roomy residence served to raise her spirits.

Mr. Polk, who was quite becoming a favorite with the family, was at the house when they returned. His presence reminded them of their more pressing difficulties. The Runner's news was evidently hopeful for once. There was a definite twinkle in his usually sad eyes. He had brought with him a package that he suddenly presented to the newlyweds and their hostess. Lady Bellingham let out a little squeal of fear.

"That's it, Mr. Polk!" Devlin exclaimed. "Where did you find it?"

"This mask is one of the artifacts brought back from the East by Sir Horace Ludlow, who was murdered some months ago. It was found by one of my men a few days after the attack on you, evidently dropped near here by the attacker. I had seen others like it when I investigated Sir Horace's murder."

Bradamant was quick to catch the implication behind this statement. "You think the crimes are connected, don't you, Mr. Polk?"

The Runner looked at her with something approaching approval. "Well, let us say I do not believe in coincidences. I believe Lord Nicholas had some business with the unfortunate gentleman?"

"Posthumously, as it happened. He was a friend of my brother's, and had carried a wedding present to me from him. It was to pick up the gift that I came back to London," Nick explained.

"Oh, I thought it was left to you in your brother's will," said Brad.

"No, he knew I was provided for. His fortune was large, but with six children ... I didn't expect him to be quite so generous as he was over the wedding."

Something sounded odd to Bradamant, but she could not yet decide what it was.

"May I ask what your brother's gift consisted of, milord?" Mr. Polk asked.

"Jewels, unset stones. I've sold most of them—the funds were urgently needed for my estate—but I managed to keep a few. I was hoping to have one or two set for my wife. There's one large sapphire that's quite lovely, and a set of peridots." He squeezed Brad's hand, with a teasing look in his eyes, remembering how she had cleverly manipulated him during the purchase of her engagement ring.

His answer disappointed the Runner. "Pity. I was thinking the nabob might have hidden a message of some sort with the gift, but I suppose that was not possible. Oh, well, it was just an idea.'' Mr. Polk's visage was mournful again. ''If either of you can think of anything that would tie the crimes together, I hope you will get in touch with me at once.''

''We will,'' they promised.

Seeing Bradamant's discouraged and perplexed expression, the Runner was moved to offer some comfort. ''I can see you are thinking this confuses the matter, my lady, but in my experience when a case seems intolerably complicated, that is when it starts to break. And remember, things are much better for his lordship now. If it had not been for the influence of a *very* powerful family member, he would have been put in Newgate long ago, and we might never have learned the truth. But we will get the villain, you will see.''

''WHO COULD IT HAVE BEEN that spoke up for me?'' Nick wondered. ''Certainly it was not my illustrious sire, as Polk seems to think.''

''Probably one of your old flames,'' Brad answered with feigned jealousy, but her mind was elsewhere.

Lady Bellingham had been silent through the Runner's visit, but now she rang for tea and inquired after the success of their house-hunting expedition.

''We haven't given our final decision,'' Brad said, ''but we'll probably take this one, despite the work that needs to be done. I wanted to look over Lady Welting's instructions before I gave the final word."

"Let me find that letter for you now, before I forget," Nick said.

The letter was a long one, not entirely devoted to business, but Brad read it all, anxious to learn about one of the few people Nick admired and cared for.

Dear Nick,

Well, our business affairs here finally seem to be almost settled. We decided to wait just a few more months so we can travel home with friends, but should finally see England at the end of May. The children are all anxious to see you, as am I.

This isn't exactly the homecoming we had hoped for. I know your thoughts, like mine, must often be with Charlie. How I wish he could have seen you again! So many of his thoughts on coming home centered on your reunion. He was so looking forward to meeting your bride, and prayed often that you would be as happy as we were.

You probably wondered how it happened. Charlie was so healthy. We had decided to stay behind a few days after sending the children to the mountains for the hot season. This was so we could spend our anniversary alone—twenty joyful years. We had a lovely celebration, with champagne and caviar that your cousin had brought over, knowing how hard to get they are here. It comforts me to know our last night together was so specially happy. By morning we were both struck down by fever, evidently caught from one of the servants. Charlie was dead within hours. My own survival was almost a miracle, but they could not save the child I carried, a stillborn son.

The children are now my primary concern, to bring them up as Charlie would have wished. I'm depending on you, Nick, to help us stay free of that tyrant, the duke. I know this is asking a lot of you, but will you purchase a home for us in London? That should help to establish our independence from Chance, I hope. All I ask is that it be large enough to house a seminary for young ladies and that it be in a fashionable part of town. For myself, I would prefer to retire to the country, but it is time the children began to take their places in the world.

This next is a little harder to ask. Silly as it seems at my age, I need a chaperon. If you know of anyone congenial, respectable, one who also knows her way about the fashionable world, please engage her services instantly.

I will notify you as soon as we arrive. The children send their dearest love, as do I. Until we meet again in London, I am

Your loving sister,
Ann

Brad tried to overcome incipient tears. "There isn't much about the house, no more than we already knew."

"We'll take this one, then."

"Yes. Lady Welting must be a lovely person."

"Ann's a good sort," Nick agreed. "She made Charlie very happy, I know."

Brad looked at the letter again, very thoughtfully. "May I show it to Kate?"

"Certainly," Nick assented, thinking he knew what was in her mind.

He was partially correct, as was borne out when Lady Bellingham instantly offered to chaperon the younger widow around town. "Just until she gets settled and can hire someone herself. And I can certainly help to introduce her to society. In fact, she's just what I need, as I can see you have guessed for yourself. To think I was worried about being bored when you two left for Yorkshire!"

"Katy, you are a sweetheart!" Nick bussed her heartily.

"That's very generous of you, Kate. But that wasn't the only reason I showed you the letter. Read it over, please, and tell me if anything strikes you as odd," Brad said.

"What maggot have you got in your brain now, my love?" Nick asked his bride.

"Something so ridiculous I'm afraid to say it. It's absolutely impossible! But it would explain so many strange things. Although, after twenty years how you could not know... Nick, did you keep any of your brother's letters?''

"No, I didn't, I'm sorry to say. You'd never have been able to read them anyway. Even I had trouble interpreting his chicken scratches, and I had had practice.''

"His writing was clear enough for you to decipher the children's names.''

"Well, clear enough so I could guess at the rest. What are you getting at, Brad?''

She did not answer him directly. "You told me all their names once, but I forgot.''

"Charlie, Nicky, George, Theo, Joe and Bertie,'' he rolled off automatically.

Lady Bellingham looked up from her perusal of the letter and protested, "No, Brad, it can't be! The very idea is simply preposterous!''

"No, it isn't. Not if you saw it, too!''

"Will someone please explain to me what this is all about?'' Devlin demanded forcefully.

"Nick, if you had heard only my nickname, and knew nothing else about me—would you think I was a man or a woman?''

"I suppose I should think Brad was a man, but...no! You cannot mean you think...''

"That Charlie is Charlotte, Nick is Nicola, George, Georgiana. Yes, yes, I believe I do. Tell me, Nick. Can you remember one single reference to those children that was specifically and peculiarly masculine?''

"No," he was finally forced to admit, in a horrified voice. "But we cannot be sure. Whatever made you even think of such a thing?"

"Little things. Stupid things. Such as your beloved and generous brother not leaving you anything in his will, 'because you were already provided for.' And your sister-in-law not asking you to show the boys around town. Instead, she asks for a woman who knows the social scene. And her choice of words—a house large enough for a young ladies' seminary? There's the way, too, that she mentions the baby she lost was a son. Surely if the others were all boys she would have said 'another' son, if she mentioned the child's gender at all. Then there's Chance. You were amazed he had not tried to interfere yet. You said he would never let go of his heir. But would he put himself out for a flock of females?"

"No, not at all. And, of course, he would know. Rendall would have run to him with the news as soon as he returned from India."

"Sir Horace Ludlow would have known, too. And he was killed."

They simply stared at one another for a moment, stunned by the revelation.

"If I am right, Nick, and Charlie left no sons, then you are the heir to Chance, a coronet and untold riches. And if that's not a motive for murder, I don't know what is."

CHAPTER SIXTEEN

"IT FITS," a stunned Lord Nicholas conceded at last. "Rendall has always hated me, always believed he was more fit than Charlie or I to fill the duke's shoes—a belief fostered by my esteemed parent. He ran back to Chance immediately after that last attempt. You know, it even explains Mr. Polk's assumption that the duke had exerted his influence to keep me out of jail. People who did not know better would assume he was acting as Chance's agent, when he really could not allow me to be arrested for anything less than a hanging offense."

"And, of course, he was the one who engineered all the rumors about you. I was a fool not to see it before. He had even started the ball rolling just before the first attempt, making sure everyone knew you were in town," his wife added.

"I don't understand," Lady Bellingham complained. "Why was it necessary to kill Sir Horace?"

"Because attention had to be centered on me," Brad explained, "on my murder, not on what was happening to Nick. If Sir Horace revealed what he knew, attention would be on the inheritance of Chance and the advantages to Sir Lucien Rendall of having Nick out of the way. Then, too, society is so peculiar. To suspect a dispossessed ne'er-do-well younger son is easy. To suspect the future—near future at that—excessively wealthy Duke of Chance is quite another thing altogether.''

''But what was he going to say when the girls arrived? Wouldn't he still be vulnerable to suspicion?''

''By the time they arrived, everything would have been long over, both of us dead and buried. If he were questioned at all, he need simply say, very innocently, that he had never really considered the possibility of inheriting, knowing that Lady Welting was enceinte when he left India. Naturally he had not heard the sad news of her miscarriage.''

Nick was suddenly and ominously still. When he spoke, it was in a voice so rigidly controlled that his audience was struck with fear. ''He killed Charlie, didn't he, Brad?''

''But he had already left,'' Lady Bellingham protested.

''Leaving behind champagne and poisoned caviar, yes. Of course he wanted to kill Ann, too, but he murdered the baby anyway. That's what happened, isn't it, Brad?''

''Yes, I think so,'' she agreed softly.

''Damn him! Charlie was worth a thousand of him!'' Devlin was trembling with rage. ''I meant to kill him for what he tried to do to you, but that's too quick, too easy. By heaven, I'll make him pay!''

"He'll pay, Nick," his wife promised. "He is going to get exactly what he wanted for you—Newgate and the long climb to the gallows. Hypocrites like Rendall can never bear the thought of exposure, and all London will know what he tried to do. And while he's in jail waiting for trial, for execution, he'll know that you have won, that very soon you will reign over the domain he killed for. We'll strip him of everything he values—wealth, power, reputation. And finally life itself."

"But we have to prove him guilty first."

Seeing a secretive look pass over his face, Brad contradicted his unspoken thought. "No, Nick, you can't keep me out of this. It just won't work."

He did not waste time with denials. "It will have to. I will not take any chances with your safety," he declared firmly.

"What good do you think my safety is to me without you?"

He had no answer for that, since he felt exactly the same about Brad.

"Besides, Nick, he won't go after just one of us. He can only afford one more try to kill us both."

"Are you two saying what I think you are saying?" Lady Bellingham asked warily, but she was ignored. Brad was still pleading with her spouse.

"You know, you're not being very flattering to me, to us all! Surely the four of us—Mr. Polk, Kate, you and I—can outwit any opponent, least of all that silly fop, your cousin. The situation will be under our control, and you will be right at my side to take care of me.''

''If anything happened to you...'' he said in a shaken voice, unable to finish.

''Whatever happens, we must be together.''

Lady Bellingham's worst fears were about to be realized. By setting a trap with themselves as bait, Sir Lucien Rendall was to be caught in the act of attempted murder.

The Bow Street Runner was called back soon to join the conference. He listened intently to their arguments, nodding in agreement from time to time. They waited apprehensively for his pronouncement.

''I said there was a connection between the attacks on you and the nabob's murder! I do not doubt but that you are in the right of it. Proving it, now that's another matter. Oh, yes, we may catch him trying to make away with you, but if he is to get what he truly deserves, we will have to prove murder, not just the attempt.''

''You are absolutely right. I hadn't thought of that. Is it possible—other than by confession?''

''Oh, I think so.'' The sad face lightened, showing signs of a hunting spirit. ''The nabob was beaten to death by footpads. If we could catch them I have no doubt but they will betray the identity of the man who hired them.''

''You think he will go to them again?'' Brad asked.

"Well, remember he is handicapped now by a broken arm. He does not dare try poison, because he will not want any comparisons to Lord Welting's death. A sniper's bullet is not sure enough. One of you would have a few seconds' warning, and for you that's too much. Yes, I think he will turn to his criminal friends again, for assistance at least. The actual deed, I think, he wants to commit himself. He will be there to gloat."

"Oh, yes, Lucien will want to gloat. And boast of his cleverness, too, if I know him."

"Good, I like confessions, they make things so tidy. Juries like them, too, in my experience. What had you considered for the trap?"

"We thought we would go to meet Lady Welting and the children at Dover, ostensibly. It's only about sixty miles, less than a day's travel. I expect the attack will come somewhere on the road where it is fairly deserted," Nick told him.

"That will make it hard to follow you."

"True, but I think more will be accomplished by following Rendall, and his associates, once he has contacted them."

The Runner looked at them both, especially the fragile gentleness of Bradamant. "I hope you both know what you are getting into."

THE PLANS TO TRAVEL to Dover were settled, despite disapproval from both Lady Bellingham and Mr. Polk. Brad and Nick meant to travel, alone, in

Devlin's new curricle, followed by servants and luggage in another coach. The journey was being proposed as a delayed honeymoon to explain their departure well before the time Lady Welting was expected. Nick was not sure who Rendall's informant might be, but doubted that any *on-dit* took longer than five days to reach Chance, if that long.

Their Bow Street Runner had gone down to Chance to keep an eye on Rendall, but within a week he was back, knocking on the door of Bellingham House early one morning. So early was it and so disreputable was his appearance that he was very nearly refused entrance.

"Good heavens! Is that you, Mr. Polk? Wherever have you been?" Brad asked, slightly disheveled from having dressed so hurriedly.

"Following his lordship's cousin, my lady. I am afraid such a disguise became necessary to appear inconspicuous in such haunts as he visited last night."

Devlin was right on his wife's heels. "So he has already tried to contact his footpad friends. Did he find them?"

"He did, milord. And I would not talk about Captain Death as if he were just any hired bravo. By rights, he is not a footpad at all."

"On the bridle-lay," said Brad wisely. She had been learning flash expressions from the Runner.

"Yes, my lady, one of the gentlemen of the road. He really is a captain, you know. Rose up in the ranks during the peninsular campaign. A marvel with horses—and with the pistols, as many a traveler has found to his misfortune. Evidently he knows a little about disguises and acting as well. Rumor says he grew up among theatrical types near Covent Garden. He is wanted for murder as well as highway robbery. Do not underestimate him. He is dangerous.''

''Tell us exactly what you've discovered,'' Nick requested once they were all comfortably seated in the breakfast parlor with tea, chocolate, ale, beef, kidneys, eggs and sweet rolls, and without servants.

Mr. Polk was too hungry to be embarrassed at being invited to break his fast at a nobleman's table. ''Well, when I got there I found that Sir Lucien had been bedridden with a bad chill since his return after your wedding. We had to keep quite a watch on the place to catch him slipping out. But finally, last night, out he runs—to a place the likes of which a gentleman such as he should not even be aware. His left arm, by the way, was in a sling.''

Nick looked a little smug at this evidence of his prowess. ''I could see the captain, and his three cohorts, but I could not get close enough to hear and live to tell the tale.''

''I don't think there is much question of what they mean to do. My cousin won't leave all the dirty work to those 'gentlemen,' who admittedly would be much more efficient. What you underestimate is my cousin's hatred for me. Rendall may hire some highwaymen to capture and hold us, but he wants the pleasure of killing me himself. Which you and your men are going to prevent.''

The Runner was not entirely pacified by this confidence in the abilities of himself and his associates. ''I have had more men assigned to the case to keep watch over Sir Lucien and Captain Death. I have others checking out likely spots on the Dover road for you to be stopped. You know Captain Death will not like that—stopping a coach in the middle of the afternoon.''

''No, not in the general way of things,'' Nick agreed. ''But if, as you say, he has a theatrical background, the captain will find a much easier way of stopping us than calling out 'Stand and deliver!' ''

''I see what you mean, Nick. We will have to keep an eye out for some trick—such as a damsel in distress.'' Brad smiled, confident, but even with this foreknowledge, none of them could look for danger everywhere it might strike.

CHAPTER SEVENTEEN

NICK WAS TRYING to devise some means by which they might hide some weapons about their persons in a way that would defy detection. So far he had only decided to place a small blade among the flowers and ribbons of Brad's bonnet.

But although the expected ambush was at the center of everyone's thoughts, the demands of everyday life must still be met. A household the size of Lady Bellingham's did not run itself. In addition to overseeing the usual preparations attendant upon any journey, Brad and Lady Bellingham were also beginning to make plans for the Devlins' eventual removal to Yorkshire. They had also to see that all the repair work and cleaning were done to make Lady Welting's new home ready for her arrival. A temporary staff had been hired to clean the house and help the family settle in.

As Brad had gone over to the huge house to check up on last-minute repairs and the cleaning operations, she had worn one of her oldest gowns, a relic of her days as chaperon to the Bagby girls. She was as exhausted as the servants after the day's efforts, but finally satisfied with the condition of the house.

"Well done, Thomas," she praised the supervisor of the servants and slipped a few shillings into his hand. "Distribute these vails among the staff, will you? I want you all to know that I am well aware everyone has done more than is usually required. You will all be highly recommended to Lady Welting."

Thomas executed a respectful bow to indicate his gratitude. "If Lady Welting proves as good a mistress as you, my lady, we shall be very happy to serve her."

"Why, thank you, Thomas. Has the carriage arrived yet? Good heavens, the weather has turned nasty!" she exclaimed, looking out the window to a dismal, wet gray world interrupted by abrupt flashes of light.

"Yes, my lady. This must be your groom now."

Even protected by the large umbrella, Lady Nicholas was pelted by rain, which was blown into her face. Wiping the drops from her face, she did not notice the unfamiliar faces of the two outriders and the man carrying the umbrella. Nor did she see the carriage's uninvited occupant until too late. A sweet-smelling kerchief was held over her nose, and within just a few moments a black void overwhelmed her.

BRADAMANT WAS NOT MISSED until the dinner hour. The threatening storm had given Lady Bellingham a migraine, and she had taken to her daybed for a long, soothing nap. Nick was in the library examining road maps of the route to Dover. He knew Brad had been puttering around in the dust and cobwebs of Ann's house and assumed her first action upon returning home would be to bathe. Only when the first pangs of hunger interrupted his calculations did he check his watch with surprise, and an inkling of fear. He rang for the butler.

"Daniels, is there some disaster in the kitchen that dinner has been set back so late?"

"No, milord. Lady Bellingham requested a tray in her room, and Lady Nicholas has not yet returned. We have been holding for her arrival."

"Not returned? Wasn't the coach to return for her some hours ago?"

"The coach did leave, milord. I thought perhaps her ladyship had other errands . . . or was waiting for the weather to clear." The butler quailed under Devlin's piercing gaze.

"Send to the house at once."

"Yes, milord." Daniels trembled. "I'll go myself."

Mr. Polk had returned to Chance, Nick remembered, and was therefore beyond immediate call—although, if the worst was realized, he might be following a different lead to Bradamant.

The flurry of talk among the servants, resulting from the butler's being sent on what seemed a trivial errand, soon communicated itself to the lady of the house. Lady Bellingham, already warned by palpitations, ran down to the library, not bothering to change out of her dressing gown and cap.

"Nick, Nick." She had to call twice to gain his attention. "Tell me at once. Is anything wrong?"

Devlin helped her into a comfortable wing chair and seated himself opposite, still clutching her hands, whether to give comfort or receive it was impossible to tell.

"We don't know for sure, Katy. But Brad hasn't come home yet, and the coach was sent for her hours ago. Daniels has gone to find out what happened."

Both were afraid to say more. Each knew Brad was too considerate to change her plans and send no message.

Lady Bellingham's lips trembled. "I should never have let her go alone."

"Door-to-door escort by a coachman and two outriders is hardly alone," Nick reminded her. "We were so sure the attack would come when we were together. If he hurts one hair on her head . . ."

They were left to worry for some hours. It was not until after midnight that a drenched and distressed butler returned bearing a message of deep foreboding.

"I am sorry, milord. They said at the house the coach had left at the appointed hour. When I asked around, however—" he had not dared to come back with less than a complete report "—it seemed that the coach had traveled with unnecessary speed in a direction leading away from this house and out of the city. Also the description of the coachman who had escorted her ladyship did not match that of any of our staff. Knowing that none of her ladyship's servants could be party to any evildoing, I continued to search for them. Finally I found our coachman and the two outriders, unconscious, in the roundhouse, where they had been taken in charge by the watch. As they were still under the influence of some drug, nothing could yet be learned from them. However, the coachman was discovered to have this note pinned to the inside of his greatcoat.''

The note was written on expensive cream vellum and addressed to Lord Nicholas Devlin. Its message was very simple.

If you make no alarm and follow exactly the instructions that will come, you may have a chance to say goodbye to your wife.

CHAPTER EIGHTEEN

WHILE NICK AND KATE were spending a sleepless night, waiting for word of Brad and further instructions, Bradamant was waking slowly and painfully in the upper room of a deserted country cottage. After a long, nauseating interval in which she was very ill, she began to take notice of her surroundings.

The men had left her alone and unbound, but there was no hope of escape. The windows were boarded up, and the single door, naturally, was locked. Nor was there anything Brad could see that could be used as a weapon, the room's only furnishings being a cot, chair and an empty chest of drawers. If only she had worn the flowery bonnet with the concealed knife—but that would have looked ridiculous with her dark old worn serge.

As Brad paced the room, she noticed that in one corner the voices from the room below could be clearly heard. She settled herself down on the dusty floor to listen.

The conversation, once she had accustomed herself to the thick country accents of three of the men, was extremely illuminating. They did not like the job.

Flash coves (by which they meant Sir Lucien) were not to be trusted. Best to stick with what you know. To this the leader (the captain?) responded that they did very well out of the last job for the cove, didn't they? Besides, they had already done the hard part. The rest was just waiting for "him" (unnamed) to arrive.

Since the arguments tended to become repetitious, Brad concerned herself with identifying voices and putting names to them. The three with the country accents, named Ned, Job and Adam, were doing the complaining, but obviously would do as they were told just the same. Captain Death, for it was indeed he, had an accent only slightly tinged with the sounds of London's back streets. For short periods he could easily disguise himself as a gentleman, or an upper-class butler or valet. Evidently all the men were cousins of some sort, and when the captain became too highhanded he was reminded that despite his years of serving the old King, he was still Martha Tindall's son Harry.

That was all Brad needed to form a plan. Now if they would only remember her existence...

The captain finally decided to go up to see if their hostage was awake. As he stood in the doorway, a single candle illuminating his rough features, he was shocked into immobility by the sound of a faintly Cockney voice asking, "Oi, don't I know you? Why, it's never...no, it couldn't be. You ain't...'Arry Tindall, is you?"

Following the captain up the stairs, the others heard and groaned. "God love us, we've nabbed the wrong one," said Adam.

"Who are you?" the captain asked, with deep suspicion.

"'Arry? It's Peg Watkins. Oh, you wouldn't remember me, anyway. I was just a kid when me mum and yours was together at the Garden. Not that Mum was in the same league as Mrs. Maria Tyndale, even when she was off the sauce—which, truth to tell, wasn't often—she was only good for low comedy." Brad blessed her late errant papa's interest in stage beauties for the memory of Mrs. Tyndale's real name, and a kindly housemaid for memories of a voice that rang with the bells of St. Mary-le-Bow. "This ain't about Elias's cut of my last 'aul, is it?" she asked timidly. "'Cause it was me got cheated, not him. Paste, that's what they were!" she exclaimed in disgust.

"No, I'm not working with Elias." Elias was a receiver of stolen goods, known for his ruthlessness in business transactions. "Come on downstairs. I want to get to the bottom of this."

"Rightyo," Brad agreed cheerfully. "Got anythink a girl can eat?"

"Adam was just cooking some eggs and ham," the captain offered ungraciously, still suspicious.

Brad sniffed the air doubtfully. "I've no mind to be poisoned, thank you. 'Ere, 'and me that skillet." She took over from an astonished Adam and began to fry the eggs in an expert manner. As she served she asked, as an aside, "What's your lay now, 'Arry?"

"My 'lay'?" he asked in his best lord-of-the-manor voice.

"You just 'appened to run off with my lady's cerridge, I s'pose." She tossed her head in a disbelieving fashion.

"What were you doing in it, I wonder?"

"An errand for my mistress, of course. I'll say this for 'er, she wouldn't make me walk in that . . . oh, so that's what you're up to. I never took you for a fool, 'Arry Tindall."

"I ain't no fool," he retorted, anger overcoming grammar. "I was paid to abduct the lady in that particular coach, and that was you."

"Thank you for the compliment, 'Arry, but I ain't no lady." So they could see. "And I was only in that cerridge 'cause my lady sent me with a message instead of agoing 'erself." Brad returned the captain's suspicious look in full measure. "You don't even know 'oo you was supposed to snatch, do you?"

"Enlighten me," he answered sarcastically, but truly needing to know.

"Lady Nicholas Devlin, wife of Lord Nicholas." Her audience was satisfyingly dumbfounded. "And you know what that means. And let me tell you, I've worked for 'im for more than a month now and, no offense, but you ain't got what it takes to beat 'im. Not you and the 'ole Royal Navy. Do you know 'ow many duels 'e fought—and won? The man ain't 'ardly human.''

Nick's name had a considerable effect on her auditors. The captain had much ado to make himself heard over their resumed complaints. Truth was, Tindall was badly rattled and trying to keep that fact hidden. He tried sarcasm again as a sneaky means of gaining information.

"I suppose you know who hired me as well," he said very nastily.

"Yus, I do. And so do they. Sir Lucien Rendall."

"And how do you come to know so much?" The captain was still nasty, but shaken.

"I listened, o' course," she answered, offended. "You really 'aven't a clue, do you? I didn't think there was a single corner of England that 'adn't 'eard the talk. Somebody tried to kill Devlin's wife before they was married, tried to kill 'em both on their wedding night—failed both times. And now 'e's failed a third."

"Do you think so?"

"Come on. Devlin's not going to come rushing to rescue 'is wife's dresser! And lucky for you 'e don't!"

Captain Death was thinking, thinking hard. He had not known Rendall's name, but he did know how he would react when he found, not his quarry, but a mere servant.

"You say you're the lady's dresser?" he asked, doubtfully.

"I'm a very good dresser," she exclaimed, her pride hurt, then more mollified. "Oh, I see what you mean. No, she don't 'ave anything worth taking, except maybe 'er engagement ring." Fortunately, Brad had not wished to risk her rings while engaged in manual labor. "But Devlin's sister-in-law is coming over from India. Filthy rich, I 'ear, and with six daughters. That means jewels, ducky, lots of 'em, and worth a little patience."

"How would you like to make a few pounds now?" the captain offered.

"What you got in mind?"

"We have to nab your mistress by tomorrow. You can lead her to us." Seeing her hesitation he pressed. "One hundred pounds."

"In advance."

"We don't get paid until the gentry cove comes."

"You risk squeezing money out of 'im, and good luck to you! Furthermore, the gentry cove ain't to know I've 'ad anythink to do wiv it. He hasn't done very well so far, but I'm not chancing 'is coming after me with a knife 'cause I know too much."

"All right, let's go. We'll plan the details on the way."

ON THE WAY BACK to town the hundred pounds in advance was revised to fifty in advance and fifty upon completion of the "correct" abduction. "Peg Watkins" would tell the Devlins that discovery of the abductors' mistake had been made when they changed carriages. They had left her for dead in a ditch, thinking she was still unconscious. However, she had overheard the name of their destination, and then was able to struggle back home.

"Devlin will rush out to capture all of you— probably taking the guards with 'im, but I'll open the French windows in the library to let you in. All you 'ave to do is give 'er ladyship a whiff of what you gave me—or I'll even do it for you—and off you go." Brad was pleased. It really was a very good plan.

But her conspirators, used to the open air, did not care to enter a house.

"Lor' love you! 'Ave I got to do all the work? I can't carry 'er out meself."

"Can't you lure her outside?" the captain wanted to know.

"After what 'appened to me? Don't be daft! Of course, if you think four strong, husky gents like you can't take care of one senile old butler and a couple of parlormaids . . . ?"

"All right," he said harshly. "Here." He handed her a small green bottle. "Pour some of this stuff on a kerchief and hold it over her nose until she loses consciousness."

"Rightyo. I remember."

The coach stopped some blocks from the square so that she could be seen walking back. The weather was still far from clement, and as she dismounted, the captain protruded his booted leg so that she landed face down in the mud.

Brad rose slowly, struck first by a momentary fear that she had been discovered, a fear she quickly transformed into a blazing anger. "Why, you bloody bastard!"

The captain grinned. "You must look as if you had been dumped in a ditch and then walked for hours through a storm."

"Stinker!" she called him, but now good-naturedly. "Miss Watkins" gave a laugh of real amusement. "Just you wait and see, 'Arry. I'll do the old Garden proud." As she marched home in the pouring rain, Brad thought Sarah Siddons could not have done better.

She went to the servants' entrance for fear one of her escorts might still be watching, staggering melodramatically to the door, and collapsed against it as if about to swoon. Due to the household upset surrounding Brad's disappearance, it was some time before her knock was finally answered by a very timid housemaid.

"Let me in quick, Polly, and shut the door behind me."

"Sweet Jesus, it's the mistress!"

Considering how liberally Brad's person was spattered with mud and dripping with water, it was a wonder she was ever recognized.

"Yes, it's me, Polly, only somewhat the worse for wear. Where's your master?"

The quick-thinking servant grabbed a kitchen towel and began to clean Brad's face and dry her hair a little. "They're all in the libr'y, my lady."

Brad ran to the library, where Nick, Lady Bellingham and Daniels remained, waiting. Nick had turned his head to the door at the sound of approaching footsteps, expecting another message from her abductors. At the sight of his mud-bespattered wife he leaped from his seat and in two strides had gripped her in a feverish embrace.

"I'm all right," she assured him over and over again, while he could do no more than repeat her name in a choked whisper.

The outcries of Lady Bellingham and the worried butler eventually brought them back to the outer world.

"I'm all right, truly I am," she repeated for the umpteenth time. "In fact, once I got over being sick I had the most marvelous adventure!"

Nick looked at her closely, near tears from sheer relief. "You have, too. Here you are practically glowing with excitement while we have been going slowly insane worrying about you."

"Oh, my poor love!" She was instantly contrite. "How you must have suffered! But you shall have some fun, too. I've brought them back for you to capture!"

"What!" Loud cries of disbelief and amazement filled the room.

"Listen to me! We haven't much time." And she explained.

Shortly thereafter, Devlin, the two guards and the youngest and strongest of Lady Bellingham's footmen were seen to leave the house and proceed in a northerly direction. About fifteen minutes later a light appeared at the French windows, and the door was opened.

The captain and two of his cohorts entered cautiously. Job was left with the horses.

"Come on. I 'aven't got all night. This way." Brad gestured in the direction with a nod of her head.

"They took the bait?" The captain wanted to be sure.

"Devlin couldn't chase after you fast enough. I tell you, I should 'ave gone on the stage." She pretended to reconnoiter the corridor to make sure none of the servants were about. "'Ere. She's in the morning room. I 'ope I didn't give 'er too much of that stuff. Though I s'pose it don't matter, not with what you-know-who 'as in mind," she said philosophically.

In a large wing chair, her face turned away from the light, sat "Lady Nicholas," limp and unconscious, clad in yellow silk and wearing a creamcolored Norwich silk shawl. With a wave of his pistol Captain Death ordered his two followers to pick her up.

"Cor, she's heavy!" one had time to complain before the "lady," played to perfection by Daniels, drew her pistol.

"I wouldn't do that," "Peg Watkins's" voice in an unfamiliar accent advised the captain, while prodding him in the ribs with a small but serviceable pistol. Suddenly Nick and his company erupted into the room, and the criminals were surrounded and overpowered.

The captain gave Brad a baleful look as he and his followers were led out the door. He shook his head and said to Devlin, man-to-man, "And she said *you* were dangerous!"

LATER, AFTER BRAD had a long and delicious soak in the bath, Nick found himself sufficiently recovered to mention, "This will change all our plans, you know."

"Yes. I half wondered if I ought to have stayed there and let you rescue me after Sir Lucien had come to do his dirty work, but finally decided we needed more control over the situation."

Nick shivered and pulled his wife's form yet closer, comfortably ensconced as they were in the big curtained four-poster. "I'll kill him out of hand before I let him threaten you again. Brad, I . . ."

"Hush, love. I know."

Still later Nick asked, "Won't he make a run for it now? After all, the captain can identify him."

"Yes, by sight, but he didn't know Rendall's name. And there's only the captain's word, the word of a highwayman, that Rendall was the one behind it. By our original plan, we would have caught them all together. Now, I'm afraid we'll need to catch him red-handed and also make him confess."

"He'll confess," Nick said decisively.

"Do we go to Dover as planned?" Brad asked, sleepily.

"No, let's make it easy for him. We'll change our route slightly and stop for a visit—at Chance!"

CHAPTER NINETEEN

"WELL, WELL, WELL! Will you look at this!" Devlin had been leafing through his correspondence at the breakfast table when one particular invitation caught his attention.

"What is it, Nick?" Brad asked, hiding a yawn. Even after sleeping most of the day before she was still exhausted and had caught a slight chill in the rain.

"A politely worded request from my revered sire to visit him at Chance immediately." He handed her the note.

"'I know you have no interest in obeying my wishes as your father,'" she read aloud with an occasional sniffle, "'but I have some hope you will respect the last request of a dying man.' Polite, did you say?"

"For the duke, remarkably so. Well, this invitation is certainly timely for us. I wonder what the old intriguer is planning now?"

"This means Rendall will be expecting us, won't he?"

"Oh, to be sure."

AT ABOUT JUST that time the strong-willed old schemer, encased in a body grown increasingly feeble, was revealing to Sir Lucien what he had done.

"Lord and Lady Nicholas coming here!" the baronet exclaimed in surprise, and then suspiciously, "Why?"

"Why? For you, Lucien. Why else?" The old man smiled nastily from the bed to which he was now permanently chained. They were all waiting for him to die, vultures and frightened rabbits. But he was not buried yet, and as long as he lived only one voice controlled Chance. As for afterward . . .

"I don't understand. Why should I want Nick and his wife to come here? I loathe him quite as much as you do."

"I know you do. That is how I knew it was you who was trying to kill them."

"What are you saying, your grace?" Beads of perspiration were on Sir Lucien's brow, which he dared not wipe. The duke was the one man who could still throw him out of countenance. Sometimes Rendall thought he hated the duke as much as he did his sons. "You are getting confused, sir. It was Lady Nicholas who was attacked."

"A clever ploy—if it had succeeded. Three failures, Lucien, three! You know, I have as little desire to be succeeded by a failure as by my radical son. But I will give you one last opportunity. If you cannot dispose of Nicholas this time, then you deserve to be left penniless."

"I shan't fail," Rendall promised with hatred in his eyes. Suddenly, looking at the decrepit form of the man who had always pulled the strings, who had always watched others jump to do his bidding, Rendall saw his way. Really, this was the best scheme of all, one that would settle more than one old score.

"Be sure you don't. For if you get caught I shall be as horrified as everyone else. Don't look to me to save you from the gallows."

"No, I know better than that." Ill as he was, the duke would probably come to the hanging and cheer. "Be assured my tracks are well covered."

"Oh? I read in *The Times* that the notorious Captain Death and his gang of highwaymen have been captured at last. There's no danger from that direction?"

So he knew about that? "None," Rendall answered with an assurance he did not feel. "They have no idea who I am." Still it was worrying not to know what had happened. The cottage was empty when he went there yesterday, and then he had returned to Chance to hear of their capture that evening. Had they been caught attempting the abduction? Or had they been unable to resist some other quarry on the road? Gossip might reveal the answer eventually, but he did not dare inquire too closely himself. Besides, there was no more time.

"I'm glad you had that much sense." The duke did not sound as if he expected much, but he would see. Oh, yes, he would see.

Rendall smiled, not pleasantly. "This time my plan will be faultless, I promise you." As he closed the bedchamber door behind him, Sir Lucien laughed softly to himself.

Behind the door, however, was an equally evil laugh.

The duke rang for a servant. "Get me writing materials and my solicitor," he ordered, sounding not the least frail, "and get them to me without anyone else knowing!"

Dying he might be, but there was not a single soul that would risk his displeasure until he was at least six feet underground.

BRAD HAD TAKEN Nick's hand in the carriage, just as she had done once before. This time, however, as they were unchaperoned he pulled her closer, seeking the comfort of her sweet embrace.

"I'm sorry for being such a poor traveling companion," he apologized. "This place always affects me like this, even without our present concerns." Suddenly he laughed. "For the first time I'm going to Chance and I don't even have time to worry about what the duke is up to! Oh, how it would hurt his pride to know that he had been relegated to second place among my anxieties!"

"Still, I wonder why he sent for us," Brad said. "I doubt he means to seek a deathbed reconciliation. Do you think he wants to get some hold over Lady Welting and the children after all—just for spite?"

"He's certainly capable of it, but on the other hand, he never has bothered with anything that doesn't directly concern Chance."

"We shall find out soon enough," she said as the old pile in all its grim magnificence came into view.

"Yes. Bleak, isn't it?" His voice was bleak as well, gazing at the building that should have meant home to him.

"Nick! I've only just realized. I'm going to be a duchess!" Despite knowledge of Rendall's motive, the concept had never before truly sunk in.

"Why, so you shall!" Nick had not really thought of it, either, being more concerned with ensuring their survival first. "And a very lovely duchess you shall be." He cast another glance at their destination, looming ever closer. "I wish I could offer you a more welcoming home."

"It doesn't have to be like this, Nick. In fact, it won't be." Brad smiled confidently. "You know, you will make an excellent duke."

He smiled. "Charlie always said I'd make a better duke than he, even when I was just a child. He never wanted all this—nor did I."

"Chance needs you, Nick, just as much as our Yorkshire place. That's how you must think of it."

"You always know how to put me in my place, darling. Well, here we are."

He stepped out and helped her to alight.

"En avant, ma cherie."

Within the house the atmosphere was more strained than ever. Chance's minor court were unaware of Nick's position as heir apparent, but instinct told them just the same that their comfortable parasitic existence was about to be changed. One look at their frightened faces and Nick finally began to believe in the duke's imminent demise. Previously, despite rumor, he had always thought the old man indestructible.

Lady Rendall was still playing hostess, as if her son did indeed own the place. Did she know? Nick wondered. *No matter what she believed, she would defend her son to the death,* he thought. In fact, the entire household was capable of supporting Rendall, at least passively, against Nick. They might not connive in the actual murder, but they would all connive to cover it up.

Sir Lucien did not appear until dinner, looking rather romantic with his left arm in a black silk sling. His stiff posture hinted that a few of his ribs might be similarly injured. Devlin certainly hoped so.

"Why, Rendall, I had not heard that you'd been in an accident!"

"With all the scandals in town I cannot believe my poor health could be a matter of interest. If you must know, I caught a bad chill, which developed into a fever. Trying to get up from my sickbed too early, I ended up tumbling down the stairs."

"Fever, Sir Lucien?" Brad asked coldly. "I hope you did not catch any of those terrible tropical fevers while you were in India."

"Yes, like the one that killed Charlie," Nick added. "By the by, Ann and the children will be arriving very soon now. Perhaps you could advise me, since you are already acquainted with them all, on any small attention they might appreciate in their new home?"

"No, nothing that I am sure you have not thought of yourself already," Sir Lucien answered smoothly.

So they fenced, all through dinner and all through the evening in the drawing room, until Brad was ready to scream. Would Rendall realize they were on to him, and panic, or would he put it down to general maliciousness and loathing? So far Nick had said nothing to pierce the armor of his overblown conceit. Or perhaps he was so sure of the success of his next attempt that it did not matter what Nick guessed or knew.

His grace the duke was too exhausted by the preparations for their arrival to receive them that evening. That dubious pleasure would have to be postponed until the following evening.

Brad let out a deep sigh of relief as soon as she and Nick were alone in their suite. "Thank God, that's over for a while. I could not have taken his chatter much longer. I was about to tell him to just shut up and and get on with trying to kill us, for heaven's sake!"

"He is pretty nauseating, isn't he? It is going to be a very great pleasure handing him over to the authorities. Oh, don't change yet, darling," he told Brad, much to her surprise. Nick usually showed considerable interest in her disrobing.

"Do you think he means to attack us in our sleep again?"

"I should think he'd have learned his lesson about that method the last time, but one never knows. No, it's not that. What time is it, by the way?"

Brad looked to the ormolu clock on the mantelpiece, but instead of communicating the hour, opened her mouth to shriek as an entire panel of the fireplace swung open slowly. Moving swiftly, Nick covered her mouth with his hand before a sound could emerge. To Brad's horror, a figure was coming out of the dark hole.

He now stood, fully revealed, hat in hand, and executed an awkward bow.

Brad was released. "Really, Mr. Polk, you should have knocked first."

"My fault, darling," Nick apologized. "I should have warned you. And, honestly, the sound of a knock would not have carried through with the panel closed."

"Forgive me, my lady. I never meant to give you a fright."

"Quite all right, Mr. Polk. It is nice to see you again. Do sit down."

The Runner perched himself most uncomfortably on the edge of a frilly boudoir chair.

"Well, Mr. Polk, have you had any trouble finding your way about?" Nick asked.

"None at all, thank you milord. Your instructions were most explicit. And I have taken my own precautions as well." He held up an unraveling ball of twine that led back to the open fireplace panel.

"You mean we have secret passages?" Brad cried out in delight.

"The place is simply riddled with them. Charlie and I used to have great fun playing hide-and-seek in them. But they can be dangerous to one who does not know them well."

"But Sir Lucien has lived here all his life. Surely he knows all the passages, too?" Brad asked.

"No, that honor is reserved solely for the eldest son, the heir. If Chance ever knew that Charlie had taught me the secret, he would be livid."

"Perhaps he means to tell you now," she suggested. "I'll wager that old intriguer made great use of them in his day."

"Oddly enough, no. I think he must have become lost in them once when he was a child, and he never recovered from the fright. He never led Charlie through the passages, but merely gave him the key."

"All of which has proved very lucky for us—and Mr. Polk."

"Yes. Have you managed to discover much in your peregrinations, Mr. Polk?" Nick asked.

"A little, enough to confirm that your suspicions are correct." Despite the open animosity between the duke and Lord Nicholas, the Runner shied away from having to reveal that the man's own father would conspire, albeit passively, at his murder. "Sir Lucien has something up his sleeve, but I do not know what. I think Captain Death's capture rattled him, but he does not see how they could have implicated him. There has been no other attempt to get reinforcements of any kind. By the way, I am not sure what the duke is up to, but he sent for his solicitor yesterday on the sly."

"Hmm. A change in his will? But nearly everything is entailed. No doubt he would love to deprive me of my inheritance, but short of proving me a bastard, I don't see how."

"I do not know what it was, but he spent many hours writing something, many sheets long," the Runner said.

"Well, he's not our first concern, so we'll just have to wait and hear what he says tomorrow night. It is time we got going anyway."

"Going where?" Brad asked.

"May I help you milord?" offered Mr. Polk.

"Thank you." Devlin handed the Runner a pile of bedclothes and began to camouflage the remaining pillows into the semblance of two bodies. "We're sleeping in the priest hole tonight, love. Less than comfortable, perhaps, but quite safe from ambush."

"I believe I shall sleep most comfortably there, thank you." And she followed Nick into the passage.

Once they were settled, Mr. Polk bowed himself from their presence and returned to keep watch over the ducal household.

CHAPTER TWENTY

LORD AND LADY NICHOLAS returned to their bed-chamber before being awakened by the servants. The precaution had proved unnecessary, but was not re-gretted. Nick was glad to see that a secure night's rest had helped remove some of the shadows under his wife's eyes. Waiting had created quite a strain for both of them.

And there was yet more waiting to do. Devlin would have liked to ride around the estate, but Mr. Polk felt this to be too dangerous. In the open, not only would they be unable to maintain close surveil-lance but it would be impossible to hear Rendall's hoped-for confession. So Nick and Brad did their best to amuse themselves by walking through the gallery and the gardens—but not the maze. They played cards; Bradamant played the pianoforte, but their attention was elsewhere.

Dinner was another disaster. Luckily neither was particularly hungry, for it was also advised that they eat nothing that was not commonly eaten by all. Poison was not feared, but perhaps some kind of soporific.

After an hour or so of desultory and dull conversation after the evening meal, Nick and Brad were frankly bored. *If this keeps up much longer,* Brad thought, *one of us will do something outrageous just for some excitement.* Fortunately, the duke's pensioners were for the most part rather elderly and preferred to seek their beds quite early in the evening. Indeed, Nick might have followed their example but that the summons from the duke was momentarily expected. Evidently the failing aristocrat was at his most alert in the dark hours of the night.

While Sir Lucien was checking to see if the duke was ready to receive them, Devlin stole a quick, comforting embrace.

"Be brave, love. That's a foolish statement—you always are. It won't be long now. Promise me you'll be careful. No unnecessary risks."

"I'll be as careful as you," Bradamant compromised.

"Now I really will worry!"

They broke apart unwillingly as Sir Lucien rejoined them.

"His grace is ready to see you now," he told them, and led the way up the main staircase and through the gallery. Long-dead Devlins watched their progress without interest. *Or perhaps there are some interested eyes on us,* Brad thought.

"I'm afraid you will find the duke much changed," Sir Lucien informed them.

"I can think of few changes that would not be for the better," Nick answered coldly. "Dare I hope that he has repented his evil ways and wishes to make his peace with God, and therefore asks my forgiveness?"

"I could not say." A careless wave of his hand accidentally released one of the papers he had been carrying. It slid toward Devlin's feet. "I'll get it," Rendall cried out quickly and nervously. Swifter still, Nick reached for the paper. He rose, smiling in triumph, but the smile was short-lived.

A triumphant smile also sat upon Rendall's lips. His good hand held taut a noose around Bradamant's neck.

"One move and your wife dies," he told Devlin cheerfully. "Really, you are so predictable! If only you had learned to exercise your wits as well as your fists!"

"What do you mean to do, Rendall?" he asked in a tight voice.

"Come now, you are not so slow-witted as that. I mean to kill you, of course."

"You don't need to kill Bradamant."

"I'm afraid I do, you know—for the same reason I tried to kill Lady Welting. There will be no son to take Chance away from me. Besides, I shall enjoy it. You were always so superior, nothing could touch you, nothing had the power to hurt you. I have that power now. What a pity you cannot be allowed to live long enough to really suffer! It was what I liked best about my original plan. To see you hang for her murder—ah, that would have been truly delicious! And, of course, when I returned from India you had disappeared. An attack on your beloved would surely have brought you forth. But by good fortune I found you anyway.''

''Tell me, Rendall, when did it start? I know you always hated me and Charlie, always wanted Chance. But when did murder become the answer?''

''You know how many years I have devoted to the duke. Bowing and scraping, saying, 'Yes, your grace, no, your grace.' Did you think I enjoyed that? But I had nothing—so I invested my smiles, my service, my submission. When he ordered, 'Go to India,' I went. And there I found your obnoxious brother, who had rebelled against it all, the heir, grown stout and successful—and the father of six girls! Girls! I was not ninth in line to inherit, I was only third. Even then it might have gone no further than wishing for a miracle. After all, you were sure to meet a violent end soon enough, by some jealous husband or in a vulgar brawl. And then I received news from my mother. She had...accidentally...come across a copy of the duke's will. After telling me for years how he wished I had been his son, the heir, he was leaving me nothing. Nothing! Not one penny was to be left away from Chance. So I began to make my plans.''

He paused and tightened his hold upon the rope encircling Brad's neck. ''Poison is very easy to obtain in the East. Even if poison were suspected, I would be far away, on the high seas. But then Ludlow arrived. He knew your 'nephews' were all girls. So he had to be stopped from talking—permanently. I had long ago found it advantageous to have a few friends on the wrong side of the law. Then I only had to kill you. But not obviously, not directly. It was such a good plan, but then I had such terrible luck. I don't know what went wrong with the abduction,'' he complained, perturbed and peevish.

''Brad convinced them they had kidnapped the wrong woman.''

''Brilliant! Worthy, almost, of myself! Such a pity, my dear, that you had the unutterably poor taste to prefer Nicholas. A woman like you deserves to be a duchess. But the time for talk is over. Keep walking.''

''Where?''

''Why, to see the duke, of course. He is expecting us.''

THE DUKE WAS INDEED awaiting them, although whether he expected such an entrance is questionable. He was sitting up in the mammoth state bed, where generations of Devlins had been born and died, resting on a sea of bolsters and pillows. To Nick, who had not seen him in months, it was a shock, despite all the rumors of his ill health. Death was in the room before Rendall entered with his murderous plans.

Wasted away and blue about the lips, he was still the Duke of Chance. His sneer still had the power to wound. "I hope you have not come to me for assistance, Rendall. I told you before, you'll get no help from me."

Rendall winced at his tone but recovered quickly, remembering his revenge. "I think you will help me, after all."

Devlin moved not a muscle at this evidence of his father's involvement, but Brad, aching for him, cried out, until restrained by the painful pressure on her throat. Staring at the selfish, evil old man, Nick said, "You know, I could almost forgive you, Rendall. This is the duke's fault. It was he who encouraged you to believe you were entitled to Chance. It was he who taught you to hate so well."

Rendall pushed Bradamant into a chair and moved behind her, never letting loose of the rope. A momentary relaxation allowed Brad to choke out, "Go, Nick, he can't kill us both at once, not with one arm."

The villain tightened the noose viciously, but not enough to kill her yet. Her fingers scrabbled again frantically, trying to loosen it, but could find no purchase.

"No!" Nick cried out in anguish. "Don't worry, Rendall. You know I will never leave her to your dubious mercies. Tell me, since you have been so generous to explain the rest, how do you mean to explain our murders? No one would believe I killed Brad now."

"No, you did a very good job of changing public opinion on that score. Quite in my own style. Everybody is looking for your enemy now, someone who hates you with every atom of his being. And I shall lead them to him. You gave the answer yourself, Devlin. The duke is to blame."

Chance roared, unafraid. "So you mean to try to pin it on me, do you? Well, you may try!"

"You know, I'm glad my earlier plans failed. This is so much better. Now I can settle two scores at once. You laugh. You think this is another failure? Oh, no. All London knows of your hatred for Nick, your determination to dispossess him. It was you, too, who invited him down here. Why else but to kill him? For years you have maintained a well-deserved reputation as a twisted schemer. They will believe it. I shall say that approaching death has left your . . . faculties impaired. My only regret is that you won't live long enough to stand trial, let alone hang."

"I told you once before, I'll not be succeeded by a fool or a failure," the duke replied. "As long as suspicion never turned your way you were safe. But you did not cover your tracks very well. I have proof. Proof of your connection with those highwaymen. Go ahead—kill Nicholas. I want to see it. But when I die you will hang for it. Fools deserve to hang." He laughed.

Full of rage, Rendall dropped Brad's noose to reach into his sling to pull out one of the duke's dueling pistols. The duke was still laughing when the bullet, fired at point-blank range, stopped his cruel voice forever.

Simultaneously half a dozen men burst into the room and rushed to overpower Rendall, while Nick dove to rescue his wife and free her from the hateful noose. He clutched her convulsively to his breast, kissing softly the bruises on her throat. Through a haze he could hear the sound of Mr. Polk's voice saying, "Sir Lucien Rendall, I am placing you under arrest for the attempted murder of Lord and Lady Nicholas Devlin, and murders of the Marquis of Welting, Sir Horace Ludlow...and the Duke of Chance."

Sir Lucien Rendall stared, unbelieving, as the gyves were fastened on his wrists. He seemed lost in a dream, until he heard the sound of Devlin's voice, demanding a doctor for his wife. Then finally his failure sank in. His screams could be heard as they dragged him to the carriage that would take him to prison. "No! No! It's mine! Chance is mine! I am the rightful Duke of Chance!"

The other inhabitants of the house remained silent behind closed doors. They would not have heard Devlin's cries; they would not hear Rendall's. Like the duke, Lady Rendall had no patience with failures. Her door, too, remained determinedly shut.

CHAPTER TWENTY-ONE

THE DUKE HAD NOT LIED. All Rendall's activities were mercilessly exposed in the file Chance had written and given to his solicitor. Sir Lucien proved himself unequal to coping with his failure. When he saw Captain Death in Newgate, he panicked for fear the gang would turn on him in revenge. Before he was even brought to trial, he forestalled the executioner by hanging himself in his cell.

Lord and Lady Nicholas left for Yorkshire as soon as Lady Welting was settled and their presence at the trial was no longer necessary. There, with solitude, peace and hard work, their wounds began to heal. Nick was now Duke of Chance, but this fact was important only insofar as it enabled him to invest endless funds into improving the estate and refurbishing the manor. Eventually, however, it was time to rejoin society and take up their new responsibilities. An announcement from Bradamant finally provided the impetus. Nick had no intention of being too far from medical help when his first child came into the world.

He had dreaded the return to Chance, but found it was no longer the place he had once hated and feared. The difference was Brad, of course. She had had the house and grounds full of workmen making renovations, and nieces making mischief.

Lady Bellingham came, naturally, full of excitement about the baby. Ann was full of comfort and advice. The sight of her brood tearing around the place kept Nick from worrying too much. His friend, Lord Ronald, was also visiting. He had come in attendance upon young Charlotte. Despite all his former resistance to the idea of marriage, it looked as though he might soon be walking down the aisle. The fact that Charlie had an immense dowry was not even important.

Bradamant and Ann had become sisters, as Nick had hoped, and found great pleasure in each other's company.

"I remember the first time I came here," she told Ann. "Nick was so upset, and I promised him it would all be different soon—the parasites would go and the halls would echo to the sound of happy, lively children."

"You've kept your promise."

"Well, I hope I have begun to."

From a distance they could discern the new duke, muddy from inspecting drainage ditches, wave to them and start in their direction.

"You know, Brad, even in India we heard rumors. Nick's a new man. This is what he was born to be—happy, useful, fulfilled...loved."

"Is he? I only know that's how he has made me feel."

Tactfully Lady Welting took her leave soon after Nick joined them. Brad took his arm cozily, despite the dirt.

"Having fun making mud pies, your grace?"

"I don't fool you, do I?" He grinned boyishly. "The bailiff thinks I go out of a sense of duty. What were you and Ann discussing so intently as I came up? Or is that question redundant? You'd think after six of her own, Ann might find babies less than fascinating as a topic of conversation."

"It depends on whose babies they are. Remember when you told me you wanted a dozen?"

"I remember every moment we ever shared. God, I can never get used to how lucky I am. The plots against us were nothing compared to what my stupid deception almost did to us."

"And mine. Seduction and vengeance—all lies. Each of us trying to deceive the other, and lying to ourselves most of the time."

"That was all the old Nick Devlin was capable of—deception."

"Is that so? Well, I hope the new Nick never changes. Because I like him very well just the way he is."

The duke and duchess were both equally disheveled and muddy when they returned home—to Chance.

WORLDWIDE LIBRARY IS YOUR TICKET TO ROMANCE, ADVENTURE AND EXCITEMENT

Experience it all in these big, bold Bestsellers— Yours exclusively from WORLDWIDE LIBRARY WHILE QUANTITIES LAST

To receive these Bestsellers, complete the order form, detach and send together with your check or money order (include 75¢ postage and handling), payable to WORLDWIDE LIBRARY, to:

In the U.S.
WORLDWIDE LIBRARY
901 Fuhrman Blvd.
Buffalo, N.Y.
14269

In Canada
WORLDWIDE LIBRARY
P.O. Box 2800, 5170 Yonge Street
Postal Station A, Willowdale, Ontario
M2N 6J3

Six exciting series for you every month... from Harlequin

Harlequin Romance·
The series that started it all

Tender, captivating and heartwarming...
love stories that sweep you off to faraway places
and delight you with the magic of love.

◆

Harlequin Presents·
Powerful contemporary love
stories...as individual as the
women who read them

The No. 1 romance series...
exciting love stories for you, the woman of today...
a rare blend of passion and dramatic realism.

◆

Harlequin Superromance®
It's more than romance...
it's Harlequin Superromance

A sophisticated, contemporary romance-fiction
series, providing you with a longer,
more involving read...a richer mix of complex plots,
realism and adventure.

Harlequin
American Romance™
Harlequin celebrates the American woman...

...by offering you romance stories written about American women, by American women for American women. This series offers you contemporary romances uniquely North American in flavor and appeal.

◆

Harlequin Temptation™
Passionate stories for today's woman

An exciting series of sensual, mature stories of love...dilemmas, choices, resolutions... all contemporary issues dealt with in a true-to-life fashion by some of your favorite authors.

◆

Harlequin Intrigue™
Because romance can be quite an adventure

Harlequin Intrigue, an innovative series that blends the romance you expect... with the unexpected. Each story has an added element of intrigue that provides a new twist to the Harlequin tradition of romance excellence.

Harlequin Books™

PROD-A-2

What the press says about Harlequin romance fiction...

"When it comes to romantic novels...
Harlequin is the indisputable king."
—*New York Times*

"...always with an upbeat, happy ending."
—*San Francisco Chronicle*

"Women have come to trust these
stories about contemporary people,
set in exciting foreign places."
—*Best Sellers*, New York

"The most popular reading matter of
American women today."
—*Detroit News*

"...a work of art."
—*Globe & Mail*, Toronto